HOMEBIRD

By Terence Blacker

Bradbury Press   New York

TO XAN AND ALICE

First U.S. edition 1993
Copyright © 1991 by Terence Blacker

Bradbury Press
Macmillan Publishing Company
866 Third Avenue
New York, NY 10022

Macmillan Publishing Company is part of the Maxwell Communication
Group of Companies.
First published 1991 by Piccadilly Press, London
Printed and bound in the United States of America
10 9 8 7 6 5 4 3 2 1

The text of this book is set in 11-point Times Roman.

LIBRARY OF CONGRESS CATALOGING-IN-PUBLICATION DATA
Blacker, Terence.
Homebird / by Terence Blacker. — 1st American ed.
p.   cm.
"First published 1991 by Piccadilly Press, London"—T.p. verso.
Summary: Thirteen-year-old Nicky Morrison runs away from boarding
school and problems at home to the tough life on the streets of London.
ISBN 0-02-710685-3
[1. Runaways—Fiction. 2. Family problems—Fiction. 3. London
(England)—Fiction.] I. Title.
PZ7.B53225Ho   1993
[Fic]—dc20   92-23536

CONTENTS

"EASY, TIGER."

    I hear my own voice in the darkness as I wake in the dead of night and the memories are there, so close that I feel I could reach out and touch them.

I see Pringle's boot coming toward me.

A shadowy figure on a rooftop, half-lit in the flashing blue light.

The broken bottle in my hand.

Dad at Waterloo Station, his eyes haunted and vacant.

Then the voices, the sounds crowd in on me. I've been watching you, Morrison. That was for him, this is for me. You are my sunshine. A police siren approaching, getting nearer and nearer, and I'm running, my breath sobbing in my chest and—

Easy, Tiger.

When you're thirteen, you can't cry out in the middle of the night. It's just not done.

So maybe, to calm myself, I'll try to read a book or switch on the telly to see some old, early-morning film, or make myself toast in the kitchen.

Eventually it goes. The past fades like a bad dream. Once again I'm just me, Nicky Morrison, a boy in his own bed in his own house, safe.

Until the next time.

1

JESSIE—DOG OF DOOM

SOMETIMES THE DANGER SIGNALS ARE THERE, BUT IT TAKES time to see them. Like my birthday last year, and the arrival of Jessie.

Friday, April 19. The dawning of my teenage years. A dark, dark day in the history of humanity.

School's over for the week. I take the bus home, that familiar route I know so well—down High Street, past the project where several of my friends bundle off, shouting good-byes to me, making plans for the weekend. Left down a quieter road, across the heath to my stop.

I don't mind this walk home. It gives me time to get used to the quiet of suburbia after the hustle and shouting of school. Past the news-agents with all the advertisements in the window. Across the road, through Masson Park, where people are exercising their dogs. And into Pierpoint Road.

What can I say about the road where I live? That it's quiet? That each of the houses has a proud little burglar alarm on its front wall? That the front lawns are as smooth and green as a row of billiard tables? That street life down our way consists of Mr. Harrington washing his car, Mrs. Zimmerman's spaniel yapping as it's taken to the park?

Anyway, it's home. I like it.

On this particular day, I'm hurrying. It's the weekend, my birthday. That morning, I've opened my cards. Tonight, when Dad comes back, I'll get my presents.

Down the path. On the door—oh *no!*—there are a couple of red balloons like I'm five or something.

I open the door, and my mum is in the kitchen, putting candles on the cake she has just bought. She looks up and smiles. "Hey, birthday boy," she says.

WHO'S WHO IN THE MORRISON FAMILY: My mum.
NAME: Mary Jean Morrison.
AGE: Forty last year (and what a crisis that was).
LOOKS: Nice. Dark hair (bit untidy). Quite slim. Motherish. Not bad for her age.
LIKES: Flowers, family occasions like Christmas, utterly gross and embarrassing hits from the sixties.
DISLIKES: Cooking, tidying up, arguments, my dad (joke).

3

HOBBIES: Gardening, finding new things to worry about.
FAVORITE EXPRESSIONS: "Just look at this room!" "And what about your homework?" "Why don't you read a decent book for a change!" "If you think I'm clearing these dishes away, you've got another think coming!" "Your teeth are GREEN!" "And WHO do you think is going to clean this?" plus several other things that end in a "!" or a "?"
STRONG POINT: She sticks up for her son in arguments with Dad or my sister, Beth.
WEAK POINT: Being a total stress case.

"Thanks for the balloons, Mum," I go. "Like embarrass me in front of the entire neighborhood, right?"

"It's not *like* embarrass you. I embarrassed you. And d'you have to end all your sentences with *right*?"

I sigh. Like Mum's the last great defender of English as it should be spoken.

"No," I say patiently. "If you had put up a sign saying THIRTEEN TODAY—HAPPY BIRTHDAY, NICKY, that would have been embarrassing. A couple of balloons is just *like* embarrassing."

I peel off a Marks and Spencer price tag from the cakestand. "Thanks for baking me a cake, Mum," I say. "You shouldn't have bothered."

She laughs. "I've got more important things to do than mess around in the kitchen."

There's the sound of a distant earthquake, a sort of rumble, growing louder and more terrifying and awe-inspiring as it approaches. My sister, Beth, is coming downstairs.

"Look what the cat brought in," she says, ruffling my hair in the way she knows I really hate. "Ready for the birthday treat?"

WHO'S WHO IN THE MORRISON FAMILY: My sister, Beth.
NAME: Elizabeth Rose (!!) Morrison.
AGE: Seventeen.
LOOKS: Put it this way: Her flesh is a couple of sizes bigger than her bone structure. Blondish, overcombed hair.
CAREER: Wants to be a (!!!) lawyer.
LIKES: Combing her hair, listening to tapes, chewing gum, reading a magazine, looking at her reflection in mirrors, sulking about how terrible her life is, talking on the phone for three hours to her friends about some nerdbrain boy.
DISLIKES: Being interrupted from doing any of the above.
HOBBIES: None.
FAVORITE EXPRESSIONS: "Look what the cat's brought in" "You MUST be joking" "Excuse me for breathing" "You and whose army?" "C'est la vie" "Takes one to know one" "Little things please little

minds" or any other items from the Dictionary of Incredibly Annoying and Mindless Clichés that happen to be in fashion.

"Birthday treat?" I ask, ducking away from her.

"Yes." This is Mum. "Your father will be home soon. He's bringing home a surprise."

"Two surprises," murmurs Beth.

Now there's something about all this that makes me uneasy—a shiftiness, like something in the air. For a start, coming home at 4:30 with a birthday treat doesn't sound like Dad. The treat I could just about believe, but 4:30? What great event could get my father back from his place of worship, the office, at that time?

His only son's thirteenth birthday? Possible. But unlikely.

Apart from being three hours ahead of his normal schedule, there are two things unusual about Dad when he arrives home that evening. The first is he doesn't make straight for the drinks cupboard (I'm not saying my dad's a boozer, it's just that the shortest distance between two points is between the front door when he comes home and the gin bottle).

And the second—

Ah yes, I forgot.

WHO'S WHO IN THE MORRISON FAMILY: My dad.

NAME: Gordon Harold Morrison.

AGE: Forty-six.

LOOKS: Tall, gray, and handsome. Beginnings of a paunch.

CAREER: Something to do with money.

LIKES: Making money, golf, making a bit more money.

DISLIKES: Mindless rubbish (anything good on television), "that horrible racket" (pop music), "wasting your life away" (relaxing), and reading his son's report cards.

HOBBIES: Listening to Bach on the CD when everyone else wants to watch TV, mowing the lawn, making money.

FAVORITE EXPRESSIONS: "Buck yourself up, old boy."

STRONG POINTS: Used to play football in the park with his son, ace at math homework.

WEAK POINT: Did I mention that he likes making money?

The second surprise is a small wirehaired terrier that's following him on a lead.

My jaw drops.

"This is Jessie," says Dad, giving the lead to me. "Happy birthday, Nicky."

"I don't believe it," I go. Call me a softy, but I've always been a total sucker for dogs. I kneel down and lift Jessie up, hold her to me. "Tell me I'm not dreaming."

When I look up, I can't help noticing that Mum has

tears in her eyes. Yup, something is definitely going on.

"What's up, Mum?" I ask. "Will someone tell me what's happening around here?"

"Good news and bad news," says Beth.

Dad gives her his dirtiest look and puts a hand on my shoulder. "We need to talk, old boy," he says.

Cut to the sitting room. The Morrison family is sitting around a low table on which there's a Marks and Spencer birthday cake. It has not been touched.

There is an atmosphere.

"Look at her," I say, smiling at Jessie as she sniffs her way around the room. "Making herself at home already."

"Probably not house-trained," goes Beth, slumped in a chair.

"Of course it is," says Mum.

"It's not *it*. It's *she*," I tell her.

Dad clears his throat and sits forward like he's chairman of the board or something. "Now, Nicky," he says in his best head-of-the-family tone. "I want to talk to you about school."

I groan. Like, Tell me something new. "On my birthday?"

"Today you're a teenager. It's a very good opportunity to take stock of the situation, assess where we now stand."

"Right, Dad." I have a bad, bad feeling about this.

"We both think that you're old enough to take more responsibility for your schooling."

We both think? It's as if I'm no longer their son but some kind of stranger. Anyway there's no stopping Dad when he's making one of his speeches.

"As you know, Nicholas, we've been rather concerned about your grades for some time. Frankly they're a big disappointment to me and—"

I tune out. This is such an old record that I know the words by heart. When Dad's little speech finally comes to a halt, I'm looking out of the window.

"My report card was a bit better last term," I go in my quiet, pathetic voice. "I was almost in the middle of the class."

"Middle," Dad says.

"Yeah. Average."

"Average." It's like doomy echo time.

"What's wrong with average?" I turn to my mother for support and she looks away. Gee, thanks, Mum.

"I'll tell you what's wrong with average," my father continues a bit more loudly. "Average means leaving school without A levels. Average means the unemployment line. There's no place for average in this day and age."

Beth stirs in her chair. "It's a jungle out there," she says, like this brilliantly original phrase had just occurred to her. We all freeze her with a look. "Well it is," she says moodily.

"Average is average," I try, staring at my dad as if to say, I suppose you've never been average in your life, have you?

"We want better for you," goes Mum, who's sitting beside me on the sofa, and I'm like, Lemme outta here. I'm definitely not happy about the way this conversation is going.

"So." My father leans forward. "We've been looking at Holton."

"Holton?"

"Yes," says Dad. "It's—"

"The school you went to?"

"It's good, Nicky," my mother says quickly. "Isn't it, Beth?"

"Yeah, I know several girls who went there. Really enjoyed it."

I'm thinking, Bring on the lie detector, right?

"It's completely changed since my day," Dad's saying. "It's got computers—"

"But it's—"

"Very good for sports," says Dad.

"And not very far from here," adds Mum.

"It's a boarding school." I manage to get it out at last. "I'd be away from home."

Mum smiles. "We think you'd benefit from a bit of independence," she says.

I look from one parent to the other, then down at Jessie, who's sitting at my feet wagging her stub of a tail. "So that's why I get a dog at last. Sugar the pill, right?"

"You'll love it, Nicky," Dad says. "I had a great time. It helped me a lot."

And I see him with his gray, tired face and his gray suit and think, Yeah, great recommendation, Dad. I stand up and say, cool as may be, "I'm taking Jessie for a walk in the park."

2

THE HAPPIEST DAYS OF
WHOSE LIFE?

IMAGINE TWO LINES OF DENSE RHODODENDRON BUSHES. Between them, there's a long straight drive sweeping up to the entrance of a great big old house, the sort of place you might be taken on a Sunday afternoon to look at pictures or a garden.

Except this is no visit. This is school, Holton.

My father's in one of his jovial moods as, one evening in early September, we roll up the gravel drive. On the way here, he's treated Mum and me to a few long chapters from that favorite old classic, Gordon Morrison's School Days:

. . . the fights in the dorm!

. . . the day he wrestled the house bully and won!

. . . the time a pigeon was trapped in the chapel!

. . . precisely what the pigeon did on the master's head!

. . . the cricket match against Wellington that was won with a six over the pavilion with the last ball!

. . . the teachers with their nicknames, Poggy White, Drag Benson, Droopy Winter, Sarge Sherwood, the matron we called—

Give it a rest, Dad, I'm thinking as we approach the big main gate.

He leads us into the school across quads, down stone corridors, past notice-boards. There are boys and girls wandering about, chatting, looking normal and happy.

"That's a good sign," says Mum.

Yeah, and where are the new boys? I'm thinking. Like, quaking in the toilets, right?

So we cross a big lawn.

"Won't be allowed to walk on the grass from tomorrow," goes Dad, who's now strutting ahead.

What? "Why not?" I ask.

"Scugs can't walk on the grass."

I sigh and walk on the grass. I don't even want to know what a scug is.

Eventually we get to a more modern building. It's Wolfe House, my new home, I don't think. At the front door, there's a little bloke with a red face and not much hair hovering about. The only ones who pay him any attention are the new boys with their parents.

"Mr. Watts, housemaster," he says, a parents-only grin on his mug, his hand stuck out. He turns to me. "And you must be Nicholas."

"Yeah." My ever-alert antennae sense a negative parent reaction. "Yes," I try. Not much improvement. "Yes, sir?" Mum and Dad smile with relief.

"Good lad," says Mr. Watts (also known as Watto, Wattsy, The Mad Monk, and other ruder names I won't bother you with).

As we make a little procession up the stairs, I like breathe in the unique atmosphere of Wolfe House—toast, sour milk, after-shave, and sweaty feet—that would soon become so familiar to me.

There's no one in the dormitory at the top of the stairs and, after Wattsy has left us, Dad and I go and fetch my trunk, which Mum threatens to unpack. Eventually I get rid of them, Mum all chipper and damp-eyed, Dad hopping around me doing the little dance that means he wants to touch me but can't quite summon up the nerve. In the end, I hold out my hand and he shakes it.

Then it's like, deep gruff voice, "Good luck, old boy."

"Yeah, cheers, Dad."

And I'm alone.

No one who hasn't been to a boarding school can know the weirdness, the loneliness of those first days. It's like you're in another world where all the things that have been familiar to you throughout your life have been taken away and there are totally illogical rules for everything.

We aren't allowed to telephone for the first three weeks, but I write a few letters. Here's my first letter home:

Dear Mum and Dad,
How are you?
How's Jessie?
How's my bedroom?
How's the house?
How's Pierpoint Road?
How are Jody, Ben, Ellie, Marlon, and all my
friends from school?
How's Mr. Harrington next door?
How's the news-agent where I used to get sweets?
How's the kitchen?
How's London?
I'm okay, I suppose.
Love,
Nicky (your son, in case you've forgotten)
P.S. How's Beth?

But this is not going to be the story of my terrible, terrible time at boarding school, big tragedy. In fact, although I'm not exactly clamoring to get back there, I have some good memories of Holton. At first it was strange but, like a battery hen or a prisoner on Death Row, you get used to it, institutionalized.

At least, most people do. There's one casualty in my year—not me, who ends up sort of retiring early, but a real casualty. Quadir. He's Asian and comes from Solihull. Like me, he arrives at Holton without a friend in sight but, unlike me, he hasn't got the survival instinct.

Straight away, it's clear that Quadir is going to have a tough time. For the life of him, he can't get the hang of the place. Not only is he Asian, which is a bit unusual at Holton, but he's extremely clever, a bit tubby, and can't kick a ball straight to save his life.

Within a few hours of being at Holton, the rest of us have clocked a few basic unwritten rules for scugs (which is the really encouraging name they give to new boys). These rules are simple:

1. Do not do anything that will get you noticed.

2. Do not speak unless you're spoken to.

3. Only make a noise when everyone else is making a noise and keeping silent would get you noticed (see Rule 1).

4. Do not answer back if one of the seniors asks you to do something, however much of a pisser it might be.

5. Keep clear of Pringle.

Almost casually, a big innocent smile on his silly face, Quadir breaks these rules one after another. The guy is a death wish on legs.

Cut to our first full day at school. We've finished morning lessons. We've played a bit of football, at which I've shown my dazzling skills. We're resting up in the dormitory, reading, thinking of home, getting to know one another. Quadir is lying on his bed reading a book that's about a million pages long.

In walks Pringle and we're all remembering Rule 5.

"Coffee," he goes, standing at the door like the Hitler of Wolfe House.

16

We all sit up and look respectful—all, that is, except Quadir, who keeps on reading.

"Who's going to get me some coffee?"

WHO'S WHO AT HOLTON SCHOOL: Pringle.
NAME: Pringle.
CHRISTIAN NAME: None.
AGE: Physical—seventeen; Mental—five.
LOOKS: Not pretty. Short red hair. A major zit attack covering his face, neck, and shoulders.
LIKES: Causing pain, terror, and despair to those smaller than himself.
DISLIKES: More or less everybody but especially Quadir.
FAVORITE EXPRESSIONS: "What you looking at, squirt?" "What you mean nothing, squirt? Calling me nothing, are you?" "I'm going to knock your teeth so far down your throat you'll need to put a toothbrush up your bum to clean them" etc, etc.
STRONG POINT: His right fist and a small, hard point of bone in the center of his forehead that nature gave him for nutting people.
WEAK POINT: A tendency to lose his temper, followed quickly by a deep need to kill or maim.
CAREER PROSPECTS: Will make an excellent psychopathic maniac.

For thirty seconds, Pringle stands there staring across the room at Quadir, the full enormity of what's happening

17

sinking in through the zits and the short red hair and into his microscopic but deeply evil brain. Then he ambles forward.

"Um, yeah, I'll make you coffee." Some spineless creep speaks up in a trembly voice—but Pringle brushes past me as he makes his way to Quadir's bed.

And Quadir keeps reading! We're all like, Does he *want* to die?

"What's your name then?" asks Pringle.

Quadir looks up and—oh *no!*—smiles.

"Quadir Begum." He puts a bookmark carefully in his book, closes it, and extends a hand to Pringle. "Pleased to meet you."

Something unsightly is happening to Pringle's face. About three-quarters of it goes pale, throwing the rest— ragged mountain ranges of red, glowing zits—into grue- some relief. He ignores Quadir's hand but picks up his book and looks at it like a gorilla trying to make sense of the collected works of Shakespeare.

"*Great Expectations*," explains Quadir. "Have you read it?"

"Great loads of ———!" Pringle swears as he hurls the book across the room. It crashes against the wall, about two feet from my friend Paul's head.

Slowly, and still smiling oddly, Quadir sits up on his bed. He looks up at Pringle and goes, "You don't like books then?"

We're just waiting for the explosion when Wattsy the

housemaster walks in. "Everything all right, boys?" he says. "Ah, hullo, Pringle." A bit more nervous, this, because even Wattsy's a bit scared of Pringle. "Introducing yourself, are you?"

"Yeah." Pringle backs toward the door and sort of grimaces at Wattsy. "Just . . . showing them the ropes, sir."

"Good man. I just need to explain about Fug-Up Extras, all right?"

"Yes." Pringle stands at the door and, before he turns to go, glances lethally in Quadir's direction. His look says, You are dead meat, man.

Quadir smiles.

A boarding school is like a small island, densely populated with morons, psychos, and loonies, and with just a few normal, nice people dotted around the place. When you're on this island, the outside world seems a million miles away and really important things—wars, riots, football cup finals, for example—might as well be happening on another planet. On the island itself, what matters are the scandals and excitements of island life, the fights, the rivalries, the campaigns of persecution.

Right now it's war between Pringle and Quadir. And it begins in earnest the very next morning, our second day at Holton.

Seven-thirty, and the dormitory is just getting ready for breakfast when in walks Pringle. He's barefoot, carrying these heavy brown shoes.

"Here ———." He calls Quadir a really insulting racist name. "Clean these."

Quadir's collecting his files together at the time. He looks across from the cupboard where he's standing and says, "My parents were told by Mr. Watts that there was no hazing in the school."

"Well, your parents aren't here now, are they?" says Pringle, not one of life's most brilliant conversationalists. He leaves the room saying, "If they're not done in ten minutes, I'll do your face some serious harm."

Now here's a problem for Dormitory B. Five of us know that the sensible thing to do is to shine those shoes but the sixth, who happens to be Quadir, isn't going to touch them. "I'll talk to Mr. Watts," he keeps saying.

And the rest of us are like, "*Do* it, Quadir."

"I'll talk to Mr. Watts."

"Wattsy won't help you," goes Paul. "Grassing on Pringle's just going to make it worse."

"You aren't going to be able to go to Wattsy every time Pringle gets at you," says Mike.

As Quadir repeats his line, I step forward. "Give us those shoes," I say. "I'll do them." Although we're all very different, there's a sort of sticking-together feeling in the dormitory. I polish away, swearing quietly to myself, and I hear Quadir muttering, "No hazing, they told my parents. I remember that distinctly."

The thing is—the rest of us had realized this instinctively—once you're at Holton, the rules are made up as you go along. There's no such thing as "fair." Any promise made outside the walls of this school is just a waste of breath.

Quadir had difficulty with this idea. For a guy who's had more straight A's than I've had "See me"s, he could be remarkably thick.

Ten minutes later, old Pizza Face is back. He looks at his shoes, shining neatly on Quadir's bed, picks them up, and inspects them. "Better," he says.

Don't, we're all thinking, don't say a word, Quadir. Just keep your mouth shut for a change.

"You should thank Morrison," he says. "He did them for you."

I'm like, Gulp.

Pringle turns slowly toward me, zits throbbing with rage. His red hair seems to be bristling like the hackles on a dog's back.

"I've been watching you, Morrison," he says to me. "And I *don't* like your general attitude."

"Gee, thanks, Quadir," I say, after Pringle has stomped out. "Remind me never to do you a favor again."

"You have to stand up to people like that."

"Yeah," goes Paul. "Particularly if you want to die."

Now here's a funny thing. Anywhere else, if someone with a rep for being a crazed psycho took a dislike to a person four years younger than him, there would be a bit of sympathy for the victim, like solidarity, but not at Holton.

21

There's a sort of vulture mentality here. No one likes Pringle, yet suddenly all the senior boys are joining in the game, goading Quadir with names, picking him for stupid, menial tasks. And, although we manage to persuade Quadir to play along with them, not to fight it, he stubbornly sticks up for himself, ignoring the insults, showing no fear, working slowly, sometimes repeating as if it were a chant from the precious little religious book that he keeps in a drawer by the bed: "My parents were told there was no hazing in the school."

Meanwhile we're praying that Pringle will get bored with this game, or find someone else to persecute.

"Just do it their way for a bit," I go one evening as we prepare for bed.

"You wouldn't understand," says Quadir, looking at me with those eyes that now have dark rings of tiredness under them. "If you let it pass, it gets worse. If you were Asian, you'd know what I mean."

We're twenty-four hours away from the moment when we can ring home to remind our nearest and dearest that we exist when the war between Pringle and Quadir takes a really nasty turn.

It's Saturday afternoon. Quadir, Paul, and I are just returning to Wolfe House from soccer, a practice game in which I scored a hat trick, Paul made a couple of dazzling, jinking runs down the left wing, and Quadir spent most of the afternoon facedown in the mud.

We shower, get changed, and make our way back to the

dormitory. The first thing Quadir does is to check the bedside drawer for his holy book, his Koran.

Religious note: To say Quadir is a bit religious is like saying Pringle is a bit of a psycho. Islam, his religion, is the most important thing in his life. He doesn't try to convert us or anything—but, at least once a day, he reads this Koran of his. It's like his way of praying.

At first, the rest of us take the mickey out of him for this. I mean, sorry about this, but my experience of religion consists of following Mum and Dad to church at Easter and Christmas, which has always seemed to me more of a social than a spiritual thing. I don't reckon God or whoever gets much of a look-in.

With Quadir, it's different. The Koran, for him, is totally sacred. He won't talk while he's reading it. We're not allowed to touch it. Even putting another book on top of it is enough to send him berserk.

Now, this Saturday afternoon, it's not there. For a moment Quadir stares at the empty drawer. Then, slowly, he sits down on the side of the bed, puts his face in his hands and, for the first time since he's been at Holton, he starts crying.

Pringle's done it. He's broken Quadir.

As you're going to discover, I'm not exactly hero material. When I read about soldiers leaping out of trenches toward enemy lines or have-a-go heroes rugby-tackling bank robbers, my first reaction is not "What a hero!" so much as "What a total idiot!"

So no one could be more surprised than I am when I

just like walk out of the dormitory, go down the stairs, and knock on the door of Pringle's room.

An apelike grunt, "Yeah," sounds through the door.

My heart thumping, I open the door. Pizza Face is lying on his bed reading a magazine. There's a pair of earphones on his cropped head and he's nodding slowly in time to some Neanderthal-type heavy metal band. He looks up meanly and asks, "What you want then?"

I go, "Could you give Quadir back his Koran?"

"What are you talking about, Morrison?"

"The book you took. Give it to me and I'll say you borrowed it because you were interested."

He narrows his red-rimmed eyes. "Get outta here, you little toe-rag. I've warned you before about your general attitude."

"Quadir's crying."

"Good."

While I'm standing there, not certain what to do next, Pringle adds, "I'll give it to him when I've finished with it." He nods in the direction of his desk where there's just a heap of papers and files, but no sign of any books.

Then I see it. The desk is too small for Pringle, and he's used four books to lift it a few inches. One of them is the Koran. If Quadir sees this, he'll be a candidate for the funny farm.

"That book," I say, giving it one last try, "is the most important thing in Quadir's life."

"I may cry," answers Pringle.

What could I do? Grab the book? Get walloped by Pringle? Go back to the dormitory and tell Quadir that his sacred book was propping up Pringle's desk?

There's no choice. I walk through to the flat adjoining the house, Wattsy's lair.

"Sir."

The housemaster's in his sitting room, watching some old film on television. He looks up, none too friendly.

"Pringle's taken Quadir's Koran and refuses to give it back."

"Koran?"

I explain the situation.

Casting a why-me sort of look in my direction, Wattsy struggles to his feet and tells me to return to my dormitory.

Apocalypse time is five minutes later.

Pringle walks into the dormitory, carrying Quadir's book in his hand like a waiter bringing in a tray. Even the fact that Wattsy is shadowing him can't quite take the swagger out of his step. He walks over to Quadir, who's sitting on his bed.

"I'm sorry to have borrowed your book, Quadir," says Pringle in a sneeringly polite tone of voice. "I would now like to return it."

His eyes fixed on the Koran, Quadir takes the book, smooths its cover once. Then, without a word, he puts it in his drawer.

As he turns, Pringle gives me his most poisonous look,

25

then brushes past Wattsy and out of the door.

The housemaster glances disapprovingly at me. Like, Don't you dare interrupt my Saturday afternoon again, right?

"Pringle has been gated for a month," he says. "I hope this is the end of the matter."

As Wattsy turns to leave, Quadir lies down on his bed and turns his face to the wall.

I shrug in the direction of Paul and Mike. "A man's gotta do what a man's gotta do," I try.

"Write your will," goes Paul.

3

PSYCHO PIZZA

GATING AT HOLTON IS NOT EXACTLY TERRIBLE; IT'S MORE embarrassing. It means you have to report once a day to a prefect who, if you're a sixth former like Pringle, is your age; you have to stay inside the grounds; and your parents are informed.

None of this worries Pringle too much. Nothing happens outside the grounds, and I've never heard anything about his parents. Maybe living seventeen years with a pizza-faced psycho has driven them away from home.

But he's annoyed. Like, really annoyed.

By Sunday morning, it's all around the house that somehow he's going to get me. The older boys shake their heads and laugh as they walk past me, or wander into our dormitory and just hang about, like sharks who have smelled blood. When it happens, which it will, they don't want to miss out on the action.

You don't live in a big city all your life without learning how to avoid bother but on this, the very worst day, I let my guard drop.

I have other things on my mind.

There's not much of a line for the telephone that morning, but it's always busy. By the time I get through to home, it's about ten-thirty.

"Oh, yeah, hi." This is Big Beth, answering the phone like I was just back after nipping out to the shops for five minutes.

"Hi," I say. "What's happening then?" To tell the truth, it's strange to be talking to Beth again. I feel almost shy.

"Same old stuff. Another day, another dollar. You?"

I pause. Where to begin? Quadir? Pringle? The fact that any moment the house goon could come around the corner and pull my head off? "I'm fine," I say. Communication has never been that great between my sister and me. "Are Mum and Dad there?"

"Er, not exactly."

"What? You mean they're out?"

"Mum's at church and Dad's away for the weekend."

"Away?" I can just about handle the concept of my mother experiencing one of her religious attacks but there's something odd about Dad being away.

"Conference or something," Beth goes, adding, "I

don't think. It's—" She hesitates, groping for the right cliché. "It's not exactly all quiet on the home front, to tell the truth."

I sense that my sister's trying to tell me something important. Waiting for her to reveal exactly what's going on is like watching someone trying to cross a stream without getting her feet wet, and the stepping-stones, her ready-made phrases, are just too far apart to get her there.

"You mean Mum and Dad?" I try.

"Right. Mr. Chalk and Mrs. Cheese."

"Beth." I'm beginning to lose my patience here. "Just tell me what—"

"It's all the time." Suddenly she's in the stream making for the other side, to hell with the stepping-stones. "Arguments. Every day. I don't know what to do, Nicky. They just ignore me. At least when you were here, you knew how to distract them but now it's getting worse and worse. I don't think he's at a conference either."

"Easy, Tiger." I feel like I'm the older brother.

"It's *not* easy," Beth wails so loudly that I have to hold the telephone away from my ear. "Why did you have to go?"

"Oh yeah." I try not to show how shaken I am by this news. "I'm miles away from home and it's still my fault. Can't you, I don't know, talk to them?"

"Not my life, is it?" Beth sighs, calming down a bit. "Takes all sorts to make a world."

"That's more like it." Before she reminds me that

it's a free country or some other great thought, I say good-bye.

Slowly I make my way down the corridor, out of the house, and through the quads and colonnades of Holton. No, it's not a free country, I think, looking around me. Every cloud doesn't have a silver lining, for that matter. And right now home does not appear to be sweet home.

The fact is, nothing Beth has told me is exactly a surprise. For as long as I can remember, my parents have been like two pieces of a jigsaw puzzle that only fit together when you force them. When I was very young, they'd laugh together a lot but all that seems a long time ago. Now Mum doesn't even make jokes about his suits and I catch a look passing between them that I really don't like. It's sort of cold—like, disappointed.

In the months before I left for Holton, the quarrels between them grew worse. It was as if, when Beth and I were small, they held back, but now that we're grown, they assume we can take it all in stride. Huh. It doesn't occur to them that the more you understand, the worse it is.

Over the past year, many of the arguments were about me.

Dad's View	Mum's View
"He's lazy."	"He's just growing up."
"He has no interests."	"There's soccer, his computer."

30

"Hasn't he got any friends?"

"He's a loner."

"It's time he stood on his own two feet."

"You don't grow up overnight."

"At Holton, you do."

"Ah yes, Holton made you the man you are."

"And what exactly does that mean?"

"You know what I mean."

"At least I made some-thing of myself."

"Yes, something—some-thing I don't like."

Etc., etc., etc.

Because Beth's tactic was to storm off and lock herself in her room, it was always left to me to divert the parents' attention from their argument by asking Dad about my homework, or simply by listening to them, looking tearful. The battle would eventually die down and, even if there was like a cold war in Château Morrison, at least further bloodshed had been avoided.

Until now.

"Hey, Nicky!" I look up and see that I'm approaching Wolfe House and that some of my friends are playing football on the green by the back door. "We need you," shouts Paul. "We're down two nil."

The last thing I'm looking for at this point is a game of soccer, but the alternative is to sit in the dormitory while Pringle prowls about downstairs, so I'm like, "Yeah, why not?"

Big mistake.

We've been playing five minutes when Pringle emerges from the house, casual as may be. For a few moments, he watches the game, hands in pockets. Then he asks, with an evil little grin, if he can play.

Coming from Pringle, this is not a question. It's a statement.

"Sure," says Paul without enthusiasm.

Pringle walks onto the pitch and, even when I see that he's not wearing running shoes but the heavy brown boots that I had once polished for Quadir, I don't get it, I don't see that he's not there for football. In fact, standing there, laughing as boys four years younger than him dance past, he seems almost human.

After a few minutes, I've forgotten all about Pringle and I'm beginning to play a bit, relax into the game.

It all happens near the other team's goalmouth. I'm in possession and up against Deverel, a big defender with a rep for innocently sticking out a leg to bring down an opposing striker who happens to be faster and more skillful than he is. The ball spins away from me as I hit the ground.

Then it's slow motion, Pringle advancing on me like a giant with volcanic acne. In the time he takes to cover the five yards to where I lie, I can see it all with perfect clarity. Why he's playing, what he's been waiting for, and what's about to happen.

I see his boot arcing back, then filling my entire vision until there's a great explosion in my head and it's like, *!!*?!wh?**bli!!hel*??')(****?*

Then it all goes black.

"Where am I?"

Yes, I really do say those words when consciousness returns. I don't say the other cliché thing, "Wha—what happened?" because, as soon as my brain cells have picked themselves up and dusted themselves down, I know that with total, painful accuracy.

Yes, my head has been used as a ball by Pringle.

"You're in the school sanatorium." Mrs. Dover, the school matron, is sitting on the end of my bed. Through one eye, I can see that she's smiling. "I'll get the doctor," she says. "He wants to get back for his Sunday supper."

Great, I'm thinking in an aching, woozy sort of way. Even when you get kicked halfway to the moon, you're taking up someone's time. The doc arrives, a skinny young bloke, all stethoscope and impatience, and, as if I'm a thing, not a person, he prods me and shines a light into my eyes.

He mutters something about my being all right after a good night's sleep and bustles off.

"That was quite a bang," says Mrs. Dover when she returns to the room.

I'm thinking, Hey, you don't say—that must be why there's a couple of porcupines breakdancing on my brain cells. "Yes," I go.

She lays a hand on my brow and it feels cool. I close my eye. This Mrs. Dover I like. She's the first person at Holton who has treated me like a human being rather than a small criminal.

Hang on. My *eye*? I snap it open. What the hell happened to the other one? Carefully I put a hand to my face. Big mistake. My forehead's twice its normal size.

Without a word, Mrs. Dover stands up and brings me a small mirror from across the room. She holds it in front of my face.

"Sheesh!" I say weakly. Talk about revolting. A great fold of misshapen blue-and-red flesh has closed over my right eye. I'm like understudy for the Elephant Man.

"Sheesh is right," says Mrs. Dover. "You have a sleep now. You'll feel better in the morning."

Now here's a weird fact that I don't tell many people. I can see the future. Not like who's going to win the Football League Cup next year but private things. For instance, I knew that it would all go wrong between my parents if I wasn't at home. I knew that there would be a problem with someone like Pringle before I had even met Pizza Face. I knew that I wasn't staying long at Holton.

Maybe it's a dream or maybe, lying there in the dark after Mrs. Dover has given me a pill, I'm thinking a bit more carefully than usual. All I know is that, by the time I wake the next morning, my mind is filled with an absolute certainty about what I have to do.

I'm going home. I'm outta here.

The day passes slowly, particularly during the five minutes when Wattsy comes to call, fussing around the bed like someone who's been told all about bedside manners but hasn't quite grasped the concept.

"Heigh-ho, Nicholas," he goes (yeah, suddenly I'm not Morrison anymore). "You can't be any good at sport without the occasional accident."

I'm like, *Accident*? but my face is in no fit state to show any kind of reaction. There's a moment's pause and I sense that Wattsy's expecting me to do the decent thing and let him off the hook.

"Yes, sir," I answer eventually. "I'll have to be careful where I'm putting my head in future."

"Good man." Wattsy smiles with relief.

"When am I coming out, sir?"

"Tomorrow evening. Or the following morning, if you prefer. Just tell Mrs. Dover when you're feeling up to it."

"Yes, sir."

Perfect.

There's only one other problem, and this I resolve when Paul and Quadir visit me that afternoon.

"I need some cash," I go.

"In here?" asks Paul.

"Don't ask why." I look at Quadir. "I need twenty quid. Minimum."

Now to say Quadir's a bit careful with money is like saying the pope's a bit religious. Only Paul and I know that he has a few notes stashed under his mattress because he doesn't trust the house pocket-money system.

"I'll pay you back," I say.

Poor old Quadir's in agony. He loves his money yet no one's stuck up for him more than I have.

"I've only got a tenner," he says weakly.

"Come on, Quadir," Paul says. "Nicky's just had his head kicked in for you."

He nods miserably, and stands up.

"And bring me my jeans and a T-shirt, yeah?" I say.

Quadir frowns, then walks off with a shrug.

"If he's not back in five minutes with the cash, I'm joining Pringle's gang," goes Paul.

But we needn't have worried. When Quadir returns, he hands me my civilian clothes, then passes me a small bundle of notes like he was some kind of really guilty drug dealer.

"Don't bother to pay me back," he croaks.

I look at the money, still damp from his palm. There's twenty-five pounds there.

I'm like, "Thanks, Quadir."

Mrs. Dover hasn't been matron long enough to discover how well boys can lie. When I tell her on Tuesday afternoon that I'm feeling well enough to check out of the sanatorium, she sees nothing odd.

"Are you sure you're better?" she asks.

"I'm fine," I say, and it's true that the swelling has gone

down and I have two eyes again. The head still aches, though.

She writes out a note on the clipboard she's carrying and puts it in an envelope. "Just give this to Mr. Watts when you go back to Wolfe," she says.

I nod, taking it.

"And Mr. Watts expects you back today?"

"Yes, Mrs. Dover," I say, delivering my brilliant lie with total cool. Fact is, Wattsy assumes I'm coming out the following morning, giving me a good eighteen hours to get away.

I get dressed, pack my pajamas, a toothbrush, and a few other things in a small shoulder bag, say good-bye to the matron, and walk out of the sanatorium toward Wolfe House. As soon as I'm out of sight, I double back through the school, up the long drive, glancing as casually as I can manage at the boys playing football on the nearby pitches. Maybe Pringle's there. Perhaps I should just walk up to him, say something so that he knows it's all his fault. Pizza Face Meets The Elephant Man. Like the ultimate horror movie.

Then I shrug. Pringle's history. In fact, Holton's history. I keep walking down the drive and soon I'm out of the gate and away.

To freedom.

4

RUNNER

ALONE ON A COUNTRY ROAD, A RUNAWAY WITH A BRUISED face, a shoulder bag, and twenty-five pounds in his back pocket yet, weird, I'm not afraid.

About half a mile away from Holton, I duck behind some bushes and change into my T-shirt and jeans. I'm about to put my dark school trousers into my bag when I remember I won't be needing them again, so I throw them in a ditch. I put my white shirt and tie in the bag.

All I'm thinking is, Tonight I see my parents, tonight we sort this thing out for good and all. I'll tell them about Pringle. The bruise on my face will do the rest. They'll think they're saving me when they ring up Wattsy and tell him that I'm never going back to Holton, but of course they'll be saving themselves, saving the family.

Back on the road, I stick out my thumb and after about ten minutes this van pulls up, driven by a guy in his teens.

"Plymouth?" I ask.

"Could be. Jump in, mate."

The man looks across at me as we drive along. "Been in a barney then?" he goes.

For a moment, I'm not sure what he's talking about. Then I remember my face.

"Playing football," I say. "Got myself kicked."

"Where d'you play then?"

"Striker."

"Glory boy, eh?"

"Sort of." I'm glad that the conversation's about football. As we approach the town, he tells me that he supports Plymouth Argyle (which I decide not to make a joke about) and in no time we've traveled the five or six miles to the station.

"See you then, glory boy," he goes, pulling up behind a taxi.

"Yeah, thanks."

"By the way," he says, nodding in the direction of my bag as I jump out. "I'd lose the school tie if I were you. It's a dead giveaway." And he gives an odd sort of wink as he roars off.

Standing there, I look down at my bag and see my Holton tie's hanging out of it. I ball it up in my hand, and casually as I can, drop it into a nearby litter bin.

Suddenly I feel a bit cold and so, as I wait for a train,

I put my white shirt back on over the T-shirt, leaving it unbuttoned and hanging over my jeans. There's no way that I could be mistaken for someone doing a runner from a boarding school.

The train breezes in, bang on time by some miracle. Humming softly to myself, I find a quiet seat, check my money (I have fourteen pounds twenty left) and, as I stare out of the window, formulate my plan.

What do you think? Go home and throw myself on the mercy of my parents, right?

You're kidding. It's all very well throwing yourself on the mercy of your parents but, after they've finished being sympathetic as you grovel around, sniveling at their ankles, they begin to change. There's heavy talk of standing on your own two feet, living in the real world. As soon as the words *real world* are mentioned, you know you're in trouble.

Say I went straight home to Mum. She's pleased to see me, yeah, maybe a bit shocked at the state of my face. Then Dad comes home, sees his boy back in the kitchen with his mummy, not standing on his own two feet, not living in the real world.

So here's my plan:

1. When I get to London, I take the underground to St. Paul's and walk to Dad's office, which I've visited a couple of times before.

2. I don't go blundering in, taking Dad by surprise when he's already pretty tense at work, but I wait outside.

3. He's tired at the end of a hard day but when his only son steps out of the shadows, his young face horribly brutalized, it's like the ultimate family reunion scene.

4. I suggest we go to a McDonald's to discuss the situation. Although he normally hates McDonald's, he's so full of unfamiliar fatherlike feelings, he agrees.

5. Over a Big Mac (I'm pretty hungry by now), I tell him everything. At the end of my story, strangely moved, he stands up and says, "It's home for you, my boy. I'll ring Mr. Watts tomorrow morning and tell him it's all been a terrible mistake and that we're taking you away from Holton."

6. Back home, it's all total happiness, like the Waltons. Mum and Dad look at each other over my head and even Beth allows herself a smile.

7. Slow fade.

8. The end.

All right, I'll admit it. I'm innocent, a stranger to the ways of the *real* world. As things turn out, I'm like way off target.

There's a sandwich bar across the road from Dad's office and it's there that I wait from 5:45 to a few minutes past 6:15. After the tube fare and a couple of Cokes I'm now down to a tenner and some change.

Then suddenly Dad's there, standing on the steps of the office, looking at his watch.

Dad. And his secretary.

At first I don't see anything odd in this. Yeah yeah Dad,

41

I'm going to myself, say good-night to her like a good boss but hurry, all right—your son's waiting to give you like the surprise of your life.

But then they walk down the steps together, turn left on the pavement, and make their way slowly, relaxed, more like a real couple than office workers, away from the underground station. She's looking up at him and he's looking down at her and I'm thinking maybe a little desperately, *Lose* her, Dad, when I catch a glimpse of his face.

It's different somehow.

I follow them, keeping on my side of the street. They amble along for a couple of blocks before turning into some kind of wine bar.

Oh wonderful, I say to myself. This is really great. It's only the most traumatic experience of my life and Dad's decided to give his secretary a drink.

I consider walking into the wine bar and going, cool as you like, "Hi, Dad, can we talk?" but I sense that this might be bad tactics.

About thirty or forty yards down the road, across the street from the bar, there's a step. I sit down on it, watching the bar all the time.

This woman, this secretary, I know her. What was her name now? Jo, that was it. When I visited Dad, she chatted to me, fetched me a Coke. I liked her—she was quite young, with curly black hair and, unlike Beth and her friends, she had discovered that she could smile and laugh and be normal. Another thing: She didn't play with her stupid hair all the time—this made her virtually unique among the girls I know.

I'm deep in thought, hugging my bag to my chest because it's getting cold now, when I become aware of two big feet in front of me. I look up to see a policeman.

"Hullo," he goes, in quite a friendly voice. "What are you up to then?"

I stand up. "Waiting for my dad." I nod across the street. "He's having a business meeting. He'll be out soon."

It sounds good, even to me. The policeman, a young bloke, glances across the road. "So what's your name then?" he asks.

"Nicholas Morrison."

Doesn't look like a runaway, I can see him thinking. Doesn't sound like a runaway either.

"What happened to your face, Nick?" he asks suspiciously.

"Got kicked in a football game."

"Funny old game." He smiles.

Hilarious, I'm thinking. "Yes," I go. "It is."

"Right, Nick." The policeman becomes more businesslike. "I'm just checking with headquarters." And before I can ask what exactly he needs to check, he's detached like a walkie-talkie from his breast pocket.

"P.C. Marselis here," he says. "Have a possible runaway. Could you check the register? Morrison . . . Nicholas Morrison." He waits for a minute or so. Then

43

the walkie-talkie crackles into life. He nods, signs off, and turns to me.

"Got any proof of identity, have you, Nick?" he asks.

I think for a moment. "Name tag," I say, pulling up the back of my shirt.

"N. Morrison," he says.

As the policeman stares at my shirt as if there's a whole chapter of a book written there, I notice over his left shoulder that Dad's emerging from the bar with Jo.

"There he is at last," I say, standing up and backing toward the street. "Thanks, Officer."

Luckily Dad's walking away from me so that, by the time I've crossed over, he's twenty yards ahead with his back to me. I glance back and the policeman's on his way, so I duck into the shadows.

They're walking really slowly now, but still I don't clock what exactly's going on. Then something happens that makes my stomach do a double flip. *Jo the secretary puts her hand through Dad's arm!* For a few yards, they walk arm in arm. Then my father says something quietly in her ear and, glancing nervously over his shoulder, releases her. They both laugh, as if at some really private joke.

Oh no. Not that. My brain cannot take this in. It's my father there, not some corny old businessman who fancies his secretary like they were in some embarrassing sitcom or something.

My first impulse is to turn and run, to scrub what I've seen from my mind, but I haven't enough money for the train back to Plymouth. Anyway I've thrown away my trousers and my tie. I lean against the wall, my heart thumping, my eyes tightly closed. Maybe, I'm thinking, maybe I can't see the future so well, because this is a total surprise.

I'm in shock.

When I open my eyes, my father and his secretary or girlfriend or whatever are nowhere to be seen. I run to the corner and there they are, ten yards down a side street, bumping against each other as they walk like a couple of pathetic lovestruck teenagers or something.

I want to scream.

Mum, I'm thinking. Those evenings when my father used to come home late from work and it was, Yeah, let's all feel sorry for the hardworking breadwinner. I swear that, if at that moment a double-decker bus had careered around the corner, mounted the pavement, and crushed the horrible lying life out of those two, I wouldn't have cared.

After a few more yards, they reach this romantic little restaurant, pause, then walk in, my father briefly resting his hand on her—on what Dad used to insist Beth and I call the "lower back."

Huh. Lower back! He should know about all that.

Through the large plate-glass window, I see some waiter guy fussing about them as if they were his best, regular customers. He leads them to a table near the back of the restaurant and my father pulls back a chair for his girlfriend. Manners were always a big deal for him.

Standing on the street, I find my eyes filling with tears. Dad. How could he? Whatever his faults, I'd always respected him. Now he was just another middle-aged man with his young secretary. This is a real champ of a cliché, one that even Beth would be embarrassed to use. I'm so upset that, for a few minutes, I forget how hungry and cold I am, how frightened.

As darkness closes in, I sit on the pavement in a small alleyway, leaning against the wall, my eyes fixed on the romantic candlelit scene across the road. I'm trying to work things out, to make sense of it in my mind.

The first time I saw Dad at work, away from the family, doing his deals, was quite an eye-opener. We were going to a film or something in the evening and, since it was the holidays, I was allowed to spend the afternoon in Dad's office, a big treat for little Nicky.

At first he tried to explain to me what he did, going into that weird language of his, which consisted of words like *debenture* and *Eurobonds*, but he seemed pretty busy, the phone kept ringing, he was glancing at the computer screen by his desk like it was a TV with the best program ever on it, so after a while I sat in a corner, sipping at a Coke supplied by Jo, Miss Ultimate Sexy Super Secretary, and just watching the action.

And, seeing Dad at his desk, in full money-making fever, as absorbed as a pilot in the cockpit of a high-speed jet, I realized I was seeing a different man here, that the Mr. Respectable, the Mr. Manners Maketh Man that I knew from home was—this is unbelievable—completely relaxed.

He swore!

It's true. Chatting on the phone to some other suit, and suddenly it was like, "Well, you can tell Smith to get his **** in gear. Otherwise I'll kick his *** from here to Threadneedle Street!" And we're *not* talking lower back here.

"Wow," I said after he had slammed the phone down like he was trying to stun some small creature on his desk. "Tough guy."

And he gave me this strange smile, half-guilty, half-proud, that I had never seen before. He looked so young. "It's the only language these people understand, Nicky."

"Sure, Dad," I said.

"If you tell your mother I swear like that, I'll kick *your* **** from here to Threadneedle Street."

We laughed in a sort of guys-together way that made me feel good and grown-up. Then he was back on the telephone giving it the old Eurodebenture blah-blah, stock option buy sell blah-blah-blah, swearing now and then, winking at me, smiling. As Beth might say, he was as happy as a pig in its own do-do.

Now, on the street, I shiver. These memories have done nothing to keep me warm.

In a funny way, that's how he is tonight. His face, like his whole manner, is changed. Different.

It's dark now. Slowly I get to my feet. I'll go home, keep quiet about what I've seen, then take the train back to Holton tomorrow. The future, I tell myself, isn't looking that black, no one's dead or anything, it's just like a dark, dark gray, the color of one of Dad's suits. My muscles are aching from sitting on the cold pavement.

Without thinking what I'm doing, I walk across the road toward the lights of the restaurant, my shoulder bag trailing behind me. For a moment I stand in front of the window, staring into its candlelit warmth. Some of the other diners look up. I see them muttering to one another but, even though my father is facing me, he's so busy looking into his secretary's eyes as she tells him some totally fascinating story that it's a while before he sees me.

Then, suddenly, Dad catches sight of me, his only son, a battered figure in a thin white shirt gazing at him out of the darkness. For maybe five seconds we stare at each other and Dad's like, Am I dreaming? Is this my guilty conscience playing tricks on me? Then he half stands up in his seat like someone who's seen the scariest ghost ever.

I fade back into the night, across the road, back down the alleyway. Nothing I could say to him will interest him as much as he's interested in Jo. I'm fifty yards away before I look back. He's standing at the restaurant door, peering down the street.

"Nicholas?" he's calling out. "Is that you? Nicky?"

I should feel sad or guilty or something but now I'm hurrying toward the underground station, a knot of anger in my stomach. I imagine you'd feel the same if you'd risked everything, doing a runner from school, to find your dad enjoying a romantic moment with his secretary.

Dad. In love. With his bloody secretary.

Excuse me while I puke.

5

BRIGHT LIGHTS, BIG PROBLEM

THINGS GET WORSE. YOU THINK YOU'VE REACHED THE bottom of the pit, that you can't get lower. Then when you get there, another, deeper hole gapes before you, and down you go again like the only place where it's all going to end is like hell itself.

Big drama, yeah? But that night was bad, the worst.

I get home at, say, ten or soon after. Just ring the doorbell, I'm thinking. When Mum has finished falling all over me, I'll tell her the Holton part of the story, and work out what I'm going to do about Dad sometime later.

But when I'm there, standing on the path, I hesitate. From inside the house, I can hear the sound of the television. I step up to the window of the sitting room and, through a crack in the curtains, I can see Beth sprawled over 90 percent of the floor, playing with her hair, and my mother on the sofa, Jessie asleep beside her. I just know if I blunder in there now, shivering, bruised, with the awful knowledge of where Dad is, that it would be the wrong move.

I can't explain this, but nothing will make me ring that bell, shatter the peace of the family. Maybe I'll turn up tomorrow, sort it all out then. Maybe not. I need to think it all through by myself.

In the park that I used to cross on my way to school, there's a little shelter. I walk toward it. On my way, I notice some bits of carpet outside one of the neighbor's houses. I take a couple of strips, then empty the rubbish from a plastic bag, making sure that nothing spills onto the pavement. I like smile to myself. Sleeping rough and I'm still worried about litter. Mum would be proud of me. The bag smells a bit but, with the felt, it will make a sort of sleeping bag.

Check that, Mr. Boy Scout of the Year.

The railings in the park are easy to climb, and luckily the local neighborhood lovers have taken the night off, so the shelter's empty. It takes ten minutes to set up my bed, using my shoulder bag as a pillow.

Lying there, listening to the distant roar of the city, I think of my family, of the mess I'm in. Tonight I don't count sheep, but think of the millions and millions of reasons why I hate my father.

1. He's a liar.

2. He pretends he's working amazingly hard when in fact he's dating his secretary.

3. All he thinks about is money.

4. He probably sent me to Holton just to get me out of the way.

5. He disapproves of everything anybody else does.

6. He's as relaxed as a plank of wood.

7. He only gave me Jessie because he felt guilty about booting me out of the house.

8. He swears and pretends he doesn't.

9. He complains about Mum's cooking when it wouldn't be totally impossible for him to do something in the kitchen himself.

10. He thinks he's so perfect because he never had any problems at school.

11. He's always finding fault with me.

12. He's a total hypocrite.

13. He drinks. . . .

I'm probably at about his thirty-ninth fault when I must have drifted off to sleep because the next thing I know is some pissy blackbird is blasting away at the top of its voice in a tree about two inches away from my head.

I open my eyes. Over the rooftops, across the park, I see the first, golden gleam of morning. Another day, as my sister would say, another dollar.

My bones ache as I sit up and bundle my bed into a nearby litter bin. It's as if, while I've been sleeping in the shelter, my mind has still been working. I know, with total certainty, that I'm never going back to Holton. More surprisingly, I realize that I don't want to go home until I've worked things out in my mind about Mum and Dad.

I need time to think.

I want to make them think.

And, yeah, maybe I do want to punish them a bit.

Who do you turn to when you're out on the street, you have eight pounds sixty in your pocket, your mind's in a mess, and you don't know where to stay?

Marlon Johnson, that's who.

At my last school, a lot of people—teachers, too—thought Marlon was a bad influence. They didn't like the way he walked, the little smile on his face when he answered a question, the sharp haircut, his easy, grown-up confidence. For them, Marlon broke the rules—not just the rules about clothes or not talking in Assembly, but the rules that say if you're black, cool, and streetwise you do badly at school. It worried them that he knew all about living wild in London, and could also get straight A's in English, math, and art. He acquired a bit of a rep as a bad influence, someone who corrupted the younger kids just by that little smile of his.

I like Marlon. Right now, as I take one last glance in the direction of Pierpoint Road, I need him.

At first, I'm heading for the block of flats where Marlon lives, but then I think better of it. Marlon's mum left home when he was six and, ever since his older sister Carla moved out, he's lived with his dad. I've only met Mr.

Johnson once, and he didn't exactly seem the understanding type.

So I wait by the street corner, sitting on a wall, aiming to catch Marlon on his way to school.

It's five to nine by the time he emerges from the flats, swinging his bag, kicking a Coke can along the road, the same old Marlon.

"Hey, guy." Marlon gives me a high five, as if we meet on the corner every morning. "What's going on?"

And suddenly I can't speak. It's weird but, after all the events of the last eighteen hours, seeing Marlon ambling his way to school, so like normal, just chokes me up. I sort of cry.

"Hey, easy, Tiger," he goes, and I manage to laugh. He looks at me more closely. "You been in a fight?"

"No." I touch my forehead, then rub my eyes as if the tears were just a speck of dust in my face. "I need your help, Marl."

He sits on the wall, as if he's got all the time in the world. "Shoot," he says.

"You'll be late for school."

"Right." Punctuality never was Marlon's strong point.

So I give him the edited highlights of the last day or so, playing down Pringle—I mean, who *cares* about that crazed Pizza Face now?—and trying to explain why I can't go home.

Marlon smiles as he hears my story. "So you're on the

street?" he says, like I've just passed some tricky exam.

"Yeah."

"Great," goes Marlon. "Let's go get some breakfast and I'll tell you what we're going to do."

"Do?" I go, matching strides with him as we make our way through the park.

"That's right." Marlon nods thoughtfully. "You're going to stay with my sister Carla. It's a squat. No one will find you there."

I swear that guy will be prime minister one day.

I've never been to Brixton before but, with the map Marlon has drawn me, I find my way to Carla's place, no trouble.

It isn't what I'm expecting. It's not a flat in a development or anything, but a big rambling house at the end of a road where most of the other houses have been knocked down. All the windows have been boarded up but there's no mistaking that this is St. Mark's Road, and the right number—a large *27*—has been painted on the door in red.

There's no bell so, nervously, I lift the rusty old knocker and bang twice.

No reply.

I knock again.

"Yeah." This is a man's voice from inside the house. It doesn't seem to be a very trusting neighborhood, since he won't even open the door.

"I'm here for Carla," I go.

"Hold on."

There's another two-minute wait, by the end of which I'm seriously thinking of pegging it down the road and back to the green and safety of Pierpoint Road.

"Who is it?" This is a girl's voice.

"Nicky Morrison. Marlon sent me."

There's the sound of about a million bolts, chains, and locks before the door opens and there's this young girl, barefoot and in a long T-shirt. "I'm Carla," she says.

I hold out a hand, which she shakes with a funny little smile.

"What time is it?" she asks.

"Quarter past ten."

"Shoosh." Carla winces like it's the crack of dawn or something. "You'd better come in."

She closes the door, pushing back the bolts so it's locked.

"Security," I say, trying a smile.

"Yeah, right."

The hall we're in is big and dark and is full of clutter, like a couple of picture frames, a sack of coal, a cupboard on its side, and a half-assembled motorbike. I can just about make out some graffiti on the walls. It's like my mother's worst nightmare.

I follow Carla up some steps and into a room which, from the piles of unwashed plates everywhere, I guess is some kind of kitchen.

"Coffee?" asks Carla, putting a kettle onto a gas ring

and lighting it with a match, which she then uses to light a cigarette.

It doesn't seem the moment to ask for a hot chocolate like my mum makes it. "Please," I say.

"So." Carla sits down at the kitchen table and takes a long drag on her cigarette. "What's the story then?"

WHO'S WHO IN THE ST. MARK'S ROAD SQUAT: Carla.
NAME: Carla Johnson.
AGE: Fifteen (claims she's sixteen).
LOOKS: Shorthaired, really nice eyes. Slim.
LIKES: Scag, Scag, Scag, and Scag.
DISLIKES: The police, meat, politicians, her father.
HOBBIES: Helping Scag with his work, painting.
FAVORITE EXPRESSIONS: "Hmm" "Take it easy" "No problem" "Meat is murder" "Ain't that right, Scag?"
STRONG POINTS: Doesn't ask too many questions, treats you like an adult.
WEAK POINT: Bit too hung up on Scag for my liking.

Over coffee, I give Carla the note Marlon gave me. She reads it, narrowing her eyes as the smoke from her cigarette curls upward from the saucer where she's put it. In fact, I think she's one of the best-looking girls I've ever seen.

"Hmm," she goes eventually. "So you seem to have

changed a bit since I last saw you. You were a real little innocent."

I shrug. Like, Mr. Modesty.

"Marlon says you've got problems at home."

"My parents aren't getting on very well."

"What?" Carla gives an unbelieving laugh.

"I think it's serious. It could be divorce."

Carla's looking at me more carefully now. "So you ran away from home, right?"

Uneasily, remembering some of the things Marlon's told me about his problems at home, I nod. "I know it sounds silly, but it's important to me."

"Do they know where you are?"

"I saw my father last night. He was having dinner with his secretary. I—I didn't talk to him."

"Naughty old Daddy." Carla smiles until she catches my expression. "So he knows you're on the run and your mum probably knows about the secretary."

I frown. "How d'you work that out?"

"He'll have to come clean, won't he? When the police ask when you were last seen, he'll have to explain. Then they'll want to know why you should run away without talking to him."

I think about this for a moment. "You're saying I've made things worse."

"Maybe not."

For a moment we sit in silence. Already I've told Carla more than I meant to.

"I'm not sure about this," Carla says, more to herself than to me.

"I won't stay for long. Just until I sort things out in my mind."

"The police will be looking for you. The last thing we need is those bastards breaking the front door down. We'll have to discuss it when the others get up."

I glance at my watch, wondering how long I've got.

"Don't worry," says Carla. "They only went to bed about an hour ago. You can have a room at the top of the house and catch up on some sleep. I'll talk to Scag when he wakes up."

I'm like, *Scag*? Who—or what—exactly is Scag?

6

HOT WIRE

MY ROOM IS A SORT OF ATTIC AT THE TOP OF THE HOUSE. It has a window with panes in it, unusual for the squat, but otherwise is a bit lacking in home comforts. In one corner there's an old, stained mattress on the floor with a blanket thrown over it. On the other side of the room is a pile of old clothes that Carla tells me belong to a girl who disappeared from the squat a couple of weeks before.

"What happened to her?" I ask.

Carla shrugs. "Found another squat. Went home. Got into some hassle with the police. Search me."

Left alone, I open the window to let some fresh air into the room, which smells of old cigarette smoke. Then I lie down on the mattress in my clothes and try to work things out in my head.

In one way, Carla's right. Word will be out about my escape, maybe the police will have been alerted. I smile as I think of the reaction at Holton and wonder whether, at last, Pringle will get his reward. Imagining Wattsy's face, all weak and panicky, I know that nothing will happen. People like Pringle always get away with it.

Then I'm back home, or rather in a totally unrealistic dreamland version of home where Dad's playing cricket with me in the park, Mum's humming some old song as she arranges flowers in the kitchen, Beth's actually smiling as she plays with Jessie.

"A week," I mutter to myself. "I'll go back in a week's time. They'll have seen sense by then."

I must have dozed off in the middle of this major cliché attack because the next thing I know there are sounds from downstairs, voices, heavy feet on the bare floor-boards.

For a few seconds, I think I'm at Holton. Then I realize the truth. I sit up on the mattress and, for some reason, I remember one of my mother's favorite sentences.

Another fine mess you've got me into.

Trying to look as if squat life is no big thing for me, I wander downstairs, my white shirt hanging out over my jeans. In the kitchen, two boys and a girl are sitting at the table, eating toast. None of them seems particularly surprised or interested to see me as I stand at the doorway.

"Cup of tea?" asks the girl, who has short-cropped hair and a sort of stud in her nostril. She's short and has the kind of smooth, round features that remind me of Beth.

"Thanks," I say.

"Mug's in the sink."

I wash out a grimy old cup, sit at the table, and pour myself a cup of tea. One of the guys, the taller and darker of the two, glances up at me with a despairing look as if I've already said something totally stupid.

I'm thinking, Gee, thanks for making me feel at home, when the girl with the thing in her nose asks, "Who you with?"

I allow a few seconds of silence to go by since slow-motion conversation seems to be the fashion around here.

"Carla," I answer.

And, hey, all three are looking at me at last.

"Carla's with Scag," says the dark-haired boy as if I'd just insulted his best friend.

"I'm a friend of her brother's," I explain.

"Something tells me"—the boy slurps his tea in a vaguely threatening way—"that Scag's not going to like this one little bit."

"Got any money?" the girl asks.

"A bit."

"How much?" From the way the three of them are looking at me, I sense that this is another dangerous question.

"Six pounds ninety."

"Oh, wonderful." This is the other boy. Like the girl, he has short hair, but he's built like a bull and his head seems too small for his broad, muscly shoulders. He looks at me with a kind of open hostility that reminds me of Pringle. "Another bloody scrounger."

"Let's have it then." The girl holds out her hand. I look her straight in the eye, like I've learned to at Holton. "We've got to buy some food," she explains with slow sarcasm.

"Carla told me we'd sort that out later," I say. With a coolness that surprises me, I stand up and with a "Thanks for the tea," I wander out of the kitchen, up the stairs toward my room.

As I walk down a corridor on the first floor, a door opens. It's Carla. "Met the gang, have you?" she asks, quietly closing the door behind her.

"Sort of."

"Don't worry about them." She glances downstairs. "They're young."

"I didn't catch their names."

"The girl's Julie. The tall guy's called John, and his friend's Pete." Carla glances at the door behind her. She seems ill at ease. "Hey, let's talk in your room. We don't want to wake Scag."

I must look surprised because Carla goes, "He doesn't usually get up until it's dark."

"So what is he, like Dracula?"

"Yeah." Carla laughs. "But without Dracula's sense of fun."

In my room, we sit on my bed and Carla tells me all

about the squat, the people who live here, and the rules of the place.

The Official Rules of the Squat:

1. There are no rules because that's what we're trying to get away from.

2. We share everything: buying (or stealing) food, cooking, washing up.

3. Anybody's welcome so long as a member of the squat vouches for them.

4. The door should be kept locked at all times as a defense against the police or the council.

5. The allocation of rooms is by mutual agreement of members of the squat.

6. There are no leaders.

Even as Carla tells me all this, I sense that there's an unrealistic amount of optimism in her version—this is the squat as she would like to see it, not how it is. Within a day or so, I've discovered the reality.

The Unofficial Rules of the Squat:

1. There are almost as many rules as there were at Holton, only people don't call them rules.

2. Shopping is done by anyone who has any money. The cooking is done by Carla or Julie, the girl with short hair. There's a rota for washing up: It goes me, me, me, and me.

3. Nobody's welcome unless everyone in the squat agrees to let them in.

4. The door should be kept locked at all times not be-

cause of the police or the council, who more or less leave us alone, but as a defense against people from other squats trying to take us over.

5. You grab what room you can and stay there until you get kicked out.

6. There is only one leader, Scag.

The famous Scag. Before I meet him, I have a bad feeling about this man. For a start, I have difficulty with his name. I mean *Scag* for some guy living on the run in a squat—is that a cliché or what? The other members of the squat, John, Pete, and Julie, seem almost afraid of him. Most of all I don't like the way Carla's eyes go soft and distanced when we talk about him. Whatever he is, I'm sure this Scag isn't good enough for her.

Considering she's a runaway, Carla's very concerned about my family. I'm for calling them the next morning, but she insists I telephone today to tell them I'm all right.

"Do it for your mum," she says. "She'll be worrying."

"Maybe."

Carla digs into the pocket of her jeans and pulls out a key. "It's a spare," she says. "Keep it while you're here. There's a telephone box on the corner."

Walking down St. Mark's Road, I'm suddenly no longer certain what to say. None of the reasons I have for running away—Pringle, Dad, and his girlfriend—somehow seems to make sense anymore, yet I know I'm right. As I approach the phone box, I find myself praying that it's out of order, or that my parents are out, or that their number's busy.

"Hullo." It's Dad and I hardly recognize his voice because normally he snaps "Morrison" down the phone as if he's the busiest man in the world. "Hullo?" goes Dad. Of course, he must be pretty busy with all the different lives he leads, I'm thinking—businessman, father, hot date for his young secretaries. "Hullo, Nicky, is that you?" In my mind I see him laughing on the street outside his office, glancing carefully over his shoulder as she puts her hand through his arm. "Nicky, listen, we need to—"

I hang up. Right now I couldn't talk to my father if he were the last person in the world.

I'm still hearing his voice when I reenter the house and walk up the stairs. From a room across from the kitchen, there are voices and, still thinking about my family, I walk in.

It's big, this room. It must have been quite a smart sitting room years ago. Now there are a few beat-up armchairs and a big television set in the corner. From the way everyone looks at me, I can guess the subject of the conversation.

"How was home?" Carla's sitting by the window. There's something about her determinedly cheerful smile that makes me nervous. It's like she's saying, I don't care *what* the others say, I'm still with you.

"Home was good," I say. "They seem . . . fine."

The dark-haired boy, John, glances up. "Got the police onto you yet, have they?"

"No."

"Nicky, there's a bit of worry that you might bring the police here," Carla says quietly. "It's very important that we're left alone."

"Right."

"Look." The girl I now know as Julie turns her back on me as if I don't exist. "I'm sure he's a nice kid and all but, let's face it, he's just a boy from the suburbs who's had a bit of a barney with his mum and dad. I mean—"

Easy, Tiger, I'm thinking to myself, who's she calling a kid? She's not exactly fully grown herself. I take a closer look at Julie, then at Pete and John. For all their swearing and tough talk, they're no more than kids themselves—fifteen, sixteen at most.

"He stays." This is a new voice, quietly authoritative.

In the gathering twilight, I now see that near to where Carla's sitting, there's someone else, his body hardly visible in the shadows, so that the words seem to come from a pair of legs in neat designer jeans and expensive running shoes. Scag, I later find out, never sits at the center of things but on the fringe as if he might slip away unseen at any moment. He stands up.

"For the moment, the guy stays," he says.

WHO'S WHO IN THE ST. MARK'S ROAD SQUAT:
Scag.
NAME: Scag.
REAL NAME: You're not going to believe it.

AGE: Seventeen.

LOOKS: About six feet, longish dark hair that some-times falls across his right eye in a Mr. Moody-Sexpot sort of way, hard-man brown eyes, strong shoulders, one earring, a big wooden cross around his neck. Sometimes unshaven.

LIKES: Breaking the rules.

DISLIKES: The world, except for Carla.

HOBBIES: Discovering new ways of getting something for nothing.

FAVORITE EXPRESSIONS: "Yes," "No." Scag's not exactly a verbal person.

STRONG POINTS: Strong, a born leader.

WEAK POINTS: Ditto (I don't trust leaders).

"He's only got six pounds ninety," Pete mutters, except he adds a couple of dozen swearwords, as usual.

"He'll pay his way. Won't you, Nick?" Scag gives me a sort of smile that, in spite of my reservations about him (in particular that name of his) makes me feel about six inches taller.

Pay my way? I'm thinking, like, paper route, washing the neighbors' cars? "Yeah, course," I say. "When do I start?"

Scag looks over his shoulder out of the window, where already the darkness is closing in. "Tonight."

"So what do I do?"

Pete smiles nastily. "You'll find out."

"Get some sleep," says Carla.

For Scag, the working day starts at 1:00 A.M.

"Let's go," he says, standing at my door, as if every night Scag and I were out on evil, money-making business.

In a sort of dreamlike trance, I get out of bed, put on my jeans, white shirt, and running shoes, and follow him down the stairs out of the front door, across the road, and down a side alley.

He's different now. At the squat, he was relaxed, almost good-humored. Now there's a swift, professional economy to everything he does.

I'm about to ask him a question but a glance at his pale, watchful face tells me that it's the wrong time for talk. It's a warm autumn night and under the neon streetlights, we walk quickly for fifty minutes.

We're in Wandsworth now and I notice that Scag's glancing casually at the cars parked by the side of the road. He leads me off a main street down a smaller alley behind a garage. There's a yard at the back protected by a high wire fence through which I can see about six cars. Scag stops. With a quick nod of the head, he goes, "Up."

I'm like, Gulp. The fence must be over twelve feet high and has rolls of barbwire along the top. I've seen friendlier-looking concentration camps on war films.

"Halfway up, there's a gap," says Scag. "Get through and undo the bolts on the other side."

Gap! It's a rathole about ten feet off the ground. My

insides turn to water as I start up the wire.

Fear is the greatest motivator ever. I climb the wire quickly and, wrenching back some loose strands, wriggle through the hole. At one point, I'm half through, upside down, looking at the ground beneath me. Then, with a tearing sound that I later find is my shirt and half my back, I fall forward and let myself drop to the ground.

Scag nods to me through the wire, as if he expected any thirteen-year-old stranger to be able to do this. "Bolts," he says. "Draw them back quietly."

As I open the gate to allow Scag into the yard, I glance at the cars. They're black, they're new, and they're BMW convertibles.

"Sit down," says Scag, and for a moment I think he's joking. Then he ducks down and pulls out a long wire from his pocket, which, crouching beside one of the cars, he inserts into the door. Within twenty seconds, it's open and Scag is inside, cutting at something under the steering column.

"Bypass the fuel cutout," he says, as if he's talking to himself. "And hot wire." He takes two wires, touches them to a third, and the car purrs into life. "Gate," goes Scag, glancing at me.

Almost sick with fear, I run to the gate and open it. Slowly, quietly, Scag edges the BMW forward until he's level with me. He nods in the direction of the passenger seat.

"Want a lift?" He gives that strange half smile.

I jump in and the car eases forward, down the side street, and onto the main road.

Idiots, guys who nick cars for the fun rather than the money, go mad when they're behind the steering wheel, but not Scag. We could be a suburban family out for a spin in the country on a Sunday afternon, he's that cool. Except it's two in the morning, and we're in Wandsworth. My heart's beginning to beat normally now. I feel elated, triumphant.

"Not bad," says Scag, as he switches on the car radio. "Not bad at all."

Maybe he's talking about the car, I don't care. I take it as a compliment and smile to myself.

We drive for thirty, maybe forty minutes. Once or twice I catch the few drivers who are about glancing at the car while we're sitting at the traffic lights, then at Scag. The strange thing is he looks the part—he has the manner, the style of someone who was born to drive a BMW convertible, not because his parents have given it to him, but because he does something flash and hard like inventing computer games, or directing videos.

We're out of London now, in the South London suburbs.

"Here we are," says Scag, driving the car up a row of terraced houses. "Follow me," he says as he gets out, leaving the car running, walks up a path to one of the houses, and rings the bell three times.

The man who answers the door is in his fifties, big with graying hair and an unsmiling mouth.

"Took your time," he says.

In reply, Scag holds out his right hand.

The man reaches into his back pocket and pulls out an envelope, which he hands over.

"We need a lift," goes Scag.

"Get a taxi."

Scag gives him this slow burn, the sort of look that tends to make people change their mind. "A lift," he says.

Swearing, the man goes back into the house and returns with a slim, balding character in his thirties.

"School outing, is it?" the man says, pushing past. We follow in our own time and, as the gray-haired man drives the BMW away, Scag holds open the door to a dark green Jaguar. He winks as I get in.

"Home, James," he says quietly. The driver calls us a few names and we're on our way.

Back at the squat, Carla cooks us the biggest, most unhealthy fry-up you can imagine. As if it's an agreement among us, we don't talk about the job at first but eat up with the quiet satisfaction of workers at the end of the day.

"So." Carla lights up a cigarette as she watches us eat. "How did he do?"

"A natural." Scag carefully folds some bacon between two pieces of white bread. "Might have been doing it all his life."

72

I give a sort of gee-shucks shrug and they both laugh.

"Well I never," says Carla. "Nick, the car thief."

Strange, but I like being called Nick. All my life, I've thought I prefer Nicholas or Nicky but now it seems to fit.

My back's hurting where the wire scraped me, tearing my shirt, but I don't want to spoil the moment by saying anything. Getting a few cuts and bruises goes with the job, I guess.

After we've eaten, Scag counts the money in the envelope given to him by the middle-aged man. There must be a few hundred pounds. He peels off a twenty-pound note and gives it to me.

"That should keep the others happy," he says.

"Fine." I pocket the note. It's the first money I've ever really earned and I feel strange about it.

"What do they do?" I ask. "The others."

"Bit of thieving," goes Scag. "The usual stuff."

"Cars, like us?"

"Don't ask, Nick," says Carla. "You don't want to know."

"They know about me," I say, more confident now. I don't like to think of Pete, John, and Julie having an advantage over me.

"Pete burgles houses," says Scag, pushing the night's earnings into the back pocket of his jeans. "John sells drugs. And Julie's a prostitute."

"Right," I nod. Like, yeah, sure, good—burglar, drug

73

dealer, prostitute, that's fine with me. "Aren't they a bit young?" I ask.

Carla gives that sad smile that I really like. "Only in years."

It must be nearly five in the morning before Pete wanders in, glancing resentfully at our empty plates.

"How did it go?" he asks to no one in particular.

Since neither Scag nor Carla answers, I say, "All right."

"Welcome to the brotherhood of thieves. When will you do it without someone holding your hand?"

For the first time since Pete walked in, Scag looks at him coldly.

"Joke," says Pete weakly. "What's happened to everyone's sense of humor?"

Scag breathes deep on his cigarette and says nothing.

7

LIVING ON THE FRONT LINE

I'M WOKEN EARLY THE NEXT DAY—THAT IS, AT ABOUT lunchtime—by the scrape between my shoulder blades. It's throbbing now and, on the gray sheets where I've been sleeping, there are bloodstains.

I look at my back in the mirror. It's worse than I thought—the long gash from my right shoulder extends about eighteen inches downward and glistens red and swollen.

Trying to ignore the pain, I sit at the table in my room, turn over the note given to me by Mrs. Dover at the sanatorium, and lay it in front of me. At first, I'm going to write to my mother but then I know I couldn't say what I want to say to Mum on paper, so I write:

Dear Beth,

I'm okay. I'm safe and looking after myself but I need to work a few things out. Dad will know what I mean. Please tell Mum and Dad not to involve the police. This is a private matter.

When I next ring, I'll talk to you and no one else.

I'd like to collect Jessie sometime, if possible, but I won't if I'm going to be tricked into coming back. I'll do that in my own time.

I hope I'm not causing too much trouble.

Love to Mum.

Nick

All right, I realize there are a few surprises in this letter. Like, why Beth? And this business about my dog—is that a cliché attack or what?

I never thought I'd say this, but sisters have their uses. Beth will understand in her own way, I'm sure. She'll keep cool.

As for Jessie, I just wanted to see her, right? Maybe she was like a bit of home for me, maybe I had this crazy idea that she was being forgotten in all the excitement. Jessie, I'm thinking, would really like this squat.

At about three in the afternoon, I hear Scag going out and, putting on my torn shirt, I go downstairs and knock on the door of Carla's room.

"Yeah."

She's sitting with her back to the door on a little stool

in front of this easel thing. In her hand is a black paint-brush. The painting that's taking shape in front of her is really good.

"Fantastic," I say, looking over her shoulder.

"Yeah, yeah." Carla's wearing this big nightshirt thing, torn jeans, and no shoes. She looks great.

"I never knew you painted."

"I sell them in Covent Garden on a Saturday," she says. "It's a bit tame beside what the others do, but I like it." She sees the letter to Beth in my hand. "Envelope and stamp, right?"

I like the way Carla's always one step ahead. "Thanks."

She opens the drawer in a table by the bed which, I can't help noticing, is in such a mess that it looks like a bomb's hit it. Carla gives me this confiding smile and says, "Restless night."

I don't want her to see me blushing, so I turn away to look at her picture.

"Your back," she says suddenly. "Nick, why didn't you tell me?"

"It's nothing," I say in my most tragic voice.

Carla's carefully pulling back a flap on my torn shirt. "Sit down,' she says, pointing to the stool where she has been painting. "Take it off."

I like it when women take control like this. Unbuttoning my shirt, I glance over my shoulder and see Carla taking some cotton wool and a small bottle out of a corner cup-board as if medical emergencies are an everyday thing for her. Stamps here, disinfectant there, I'm thinking to myself—some squatter she is. "You're very organized," I say.

"Someone's got to be." She sits on the side of the bed. "Bring that stool over here."

Laying one cool, dark hand on my shoulder, she dabs at my cut with the cotton wool and disinfectant. It's painful but in a nice, reassuring way that reminds me of times I used to fall off my bicycle and have my knees repaired by Mum when I was a kid.

"Aaah." I arch my back as the cut stings under the disinfectant. I can't help it but I'm laughing at the pain. Carla laughs, too.

"Stop wriggling," she says. "You're a wimp, Nick."

"It's bloody agony."

"Florence Nightingale strikes again." Suddenly Scag's standing at the door, looking at us. He's smiling but there's something strained about him that wasn't there last night.

"Nick cut himself—" says Carla.

"On the wire," I add.

Scag takes a closer look at my back. "You'll live," he says.

"Sure." Suddenly I feel awkward being in his room. I notice Carla's taken her hand off my shoulder. After a couple of moments, she gets up and says, "There you are then." She reaches for my shirt. "This is no good," she says—except she doesn't say "no good" but uses a swear-word. I notice that, whenever Scag's around, she tries to act tougher than she is.

"I'll have to sew it up," I tell her. "It's the only one I've got."

Carla opens a drawer and hands me a black T-shirt. "We're about the same size," she says. "Let me have it back sometime."

I return to my room and put on the T-shirt. It smells faintly of Carla. Fact is, I don't mind that one bit.

A week and a half pass like it was a day. Soon I get into the rhythm of the squat, going to bed when other people are going to work, getting up after lunch, eating whenever you feel like it. Every night, I'm out to work with Scag.

As I get to know him a bit better, I find there's something restless about Scag. He only seems truly happy when he's on a job, either looking out for likely cars or garages or actually doing the deed. After three or four nights, the excitement begins to fade for me. I keep a lookout or do a bit of climbing. Scag shows me how to start a car without keys. Although we're like partners now, I'm wary of him. Now and then I catch him giving me this look—not entirely friendly, but watchful, as if it's only a matter of time before I do something wrong.

Thoughts of home sneak up on me at the most unlikely of times. I'll be standing in the shadows on the street and suddenly I'll see Mum in the kitchen or wonder whether Dad's still seeing that secretary of his. Then I snap out of it.

The best part of my new life is that I don't have much time to think about the future.

Scag, I notice, has given up paying me. Every time we deliver a car to the address in South London, he receives an envelope bulging with cash, but now he keeps it to himself. I don't mind—I'm not in this for the money.

He, or Carla, must be paying something for my food, though, because the others never mention it again.

My relations with Julie, Pete, and John do not improve. Julie, in particular, treats me as if I've just crawled out from under a stone.

Her moods bewilder me at first. Some nights she's loud and happy, laughing at virtually anything, the next she's pale, with great rings under her eyes and seems almost unable to speak she's so depressed.

Maybe it's her work. Maybe it's the pills I've seen her taking. I don't want to know.

Funnily enough, it's Julie who notices the change in me the day I ring home and talk to Beth.

It's a Friday afternoon when I leave the house and walk to the telephone box on the corner.

Twice my father answers. I hang up without a word. The third time, they get the message—it's Beth on the line.

"Hi," I go. "It's me."

"Where are you, Nicky?" My sister sounds really scared.

"Around. I'm okay."

"Listen," goes Beth. "I don't know what all this is about but you've got to come back. We're all dead worried about you. Dad hasn't been to work all week."

I'm thinking like, Big deal, but can't seem to say anything.

"If it's about school, Nicky," Beth's going, "just come back and talk about it. You're making us all ill with worry."

"Have you told the police?"

There's a pause and I can hear voices in the background. "Of course, we had to. Listen, Mum wants to know if you're eating all right. She's here if you want to—"

Slowly I replace the receiver. I'm not stupid. I've seen the films. Calls can be traced if you talk for too long.

Something strange is happening when I get back to the squat—Julie is doing the washing up. This is like saying "Scag is out mowing the lawn" or maybe "Pete is doing a door-to-door collection for the local church." Unusual, to say the least.

"Hi, Junior," she goes as I walk in.

Under normal circumstances, I don't answer to this name she's given me—strange as it may seem, I'm not happy about the idea of being patronized by a fifteen-year-old prostitute—but right now my defenses are down.

"Hi," I say. "Can I help?"

"Sure, Junior."

There's a dirty old tea cloth on the table. I pick it up and start doing some drying up. It reminds me of being at home, in the kitchen with Mum or Beth.

Julie's humming this tune. It's such a terrible noise

that, although I'm feeling down, I smile.

"Nice song," I go.

"Cheers," says Julie, giving me a sideward glance. "So when are you going to be on your way, Junior?" she asks.

"Dunno. When I've sorted things out."

She sings a bit more. "I'd make it soon if I were you."

"Yeah?" Like, Thanks for the advice, Julie.

"Your folks will be worried."

There's one thing I know about Julie, and that is that she wouldn't give a thought for me or my family. "They're okay," I say. "I just spoke to my sister. It's all under control."

"Listen." Julie glances toward the door as if to check we're alone. "You don't know Scag like I know him. When you meet him, he's like Mr. Concerned, Mr. Generous. Then he changes. He's a bad enemy, Junior. He smiles, but he's dangerous."

"I can look after myself."

"There's only one thing in the world he really cares about, and that's Carla. She keeps him from doing something really stupid. He loves her, right." Julie's looking at me, her slate gray eyes unblinking and hostile.

I shrug. "So what's that got to do with me?"

"Quite the little innocent, eh, Junior?" She goes back to washing out a mug. "Don't say I didn't warn you."

At the time, it's true, I have no idea what Julie's on about. I just put this heavy warning down to one of her weird moods.

"Where's Scag now?" I ask.

"He's in bed with Carla." Julie gives a cold little laugh. "Where else?"

Fact is, Julie's advice is good. Although she probably has her own selfish reasons for wanting me out of the squat, her instinct that there's trouble on the way is right.

Not that I see it that way at the time. I'm thinking, a few more days and I'll be home, having worked things out in my mind. I imagine this big man-to-man scene with my father, perhaps after Mum and Beth have gone to bed.

ME: Look, Dad, you know why I did what I did. I'll say nothing to Mum if you face up to your family responsibilities.

FATHER: I hadn't realized you felt so strongly about it, Nicky.

ME: Nick. I'm Nick now.

FATHER: Sorry, Nick.

ME: So it's agreed. You spend more time with Mum and I promise never to run away again.

FATHER: Yes, Nick. Agreed. Now about school—

ME (giving him a Scag-like smoldering look): What about school?

FATHER (nervously): Er, nothing. You just tell me what you'd like to do.

It's a pathetic dream of course. Two days, maybe three,

into my life on the run, I might have been able to go back and face my father but now it's all gone too far—or at least it has after the events of that weekend.

Carla has noticed that, after calling home, I'm quieter than usual. On the Friday night, Scag's out meeting someone, the other three are working, so Carla and I are alone watching a film on the television.

Except I'm not concentrating on the film but thinking of home and how different Beth sounded on the telephone.

"I think I'll get my dog tomorrow," I say, as casually as I can manage.

"Yeah?" Carla looks pleased. She likes animals and I've told her all about Jessie.

"Will the others mind?"

"Not if you square it with Scag," says Carla. "I'll tell him tonight when he gets back.

"Quite the homebird at heart." She smiles. "You're missing them all."

I shrug. "I just want my dog. I'll wait until my sister takes her for a walk. Then I'll explain to her that I need Jessie and that I'll be back home in a couple of days."

"She'll accept that?" Carla's not looking at the screen anymore.

"She'll have to."

"I'll come with you," she says. "Your sister might be being watched. The police are clever like that."

"Thanks."

84

And Carla gives me this funny look, which I don't understand at the time. "It'll be my pleasure," she says.

The next morning, Carla bangs on my door to wake me. It's nine-thirty. The first time we've been up before lunch since I've been here.

Our plan is this:

1. From the far side of Masson Park, we wait for Beth, who would never take Jessie out before ten on a Saturday.

2. I point her out to Carla.

3. She checks around the edge of the park to see whether Beth is being watched or followed.

4. I move in, tell Beth we need Jessie.

5. We peg it out of there.

I'm expecting the sight of the park to make me feel homesick but, the fact is, I'm too engrossed in my conversation with Carla to notice anything much. Now that we're away from the squat, she seems more relaxed.

For like ten or fifteen minutes, we sit under a tree talking about this and that—her home, Marlon, how she met Scag. She's smoking a cigarette, I'm chewing gum; it's so nice I find myself hoping that Beth and Jessie will wait for a while before making their appearance.

"So that's how you ended up as a squatter," I'm saying.

"Yeah, me, the housemother, the gangster's moll. I can't believe it really."

"If it wasn't for Scag, you wouldn't be there, right?"

"I doubt it."

I still have no idea where the next question came from, how it hijacked my brain. "Are you—" I hesitate. "Are you like deeply in love with him."

"Deeply?" She laughs. "I don't know about deeply."

There's something about Carla's manner that suggests it would be a bad idea to press this further.

Carla's staring across the park. "I think that dog of yours is going to have to wait," she says quietly.

I follow the direction of her eyes. Near the dog exercise area there's a bench on which a young guy with a mustache is sitting, reading a paper.

"Rozzer," goes Carla.

"How d'you know he's a policeman?" I ask but, as I speak, the man looks over his paper in our direction.

"Here, quick," Carla says, holding out her hand. "He's seen us."

And suddenly I'm walking hand in hand through the park with Carla.

"Good thinking, huh?" she says. "Runaways don't wander about with their girlfriends."

"Sure," I say faintly. "Young love, right."

Carla laughs.

I take a peek over her shoulder and notice that the man is once again reading his paper. We turn out of the park, but Carla's still holding my hand. Around a corner and she stops, like someone who's forgotten something.

"That was for him." She steps closer. "This is for me." And, before I can say anything, she's kissing me, not one of those gross eat-you-alive numbers you see on film but not like a sister either—on the lips, just leaning against me in a way that's more than friendly. At that moment, I've forgotten about home and school and Scag, I'm so happy.

Then, just as I'm wondering if I should be doing something with my hands, she breaks away and marches off down the street, singing out, "Shame about the dog, eh?"

"Yeah," I say, following her, my heart still thumping.

Sometime later, when we're emerging from the Brixton underground after a journey passed in almost complete silence, Carla says, "I shouldn't have done that, Nick."

I shrug in an I-can-take-it-or-leave-it way. "It was nice."

"Don't get the wrong idea," she says, walking quickly now. "I'm with Scag, right."

"Just good friends," I say, finding the right Beth cliché for the moment.

But Carla doesn't seem to hear.

8

PARTY TIME

SOMETIMES I THINK I'M ONE OF THOSE PEOPLE WHO RUB other people the wrong way, almost without trying.

Like at home, I annoy my dad so much that he decides to send me to Holton.

At Holton, Pringle decides that, of all the scugs at Wolfe, I'm the one that needs my face kicked in.

On the run, the first thing I do is discover like the biggest secret in my father's life.

By some miracle, the person who runs the squat lets me work with him. And what happens? I get involved with his girlfriend.

The fact is, until now I've no idea that the situation with Carla is getting dangerous. We're friends. We talk. We get on. Does that make me some kind of love rival to Scag of all people? Ridiculous.

All right, maybe not quite so ridiculous. It's true that I like Carla a lot, that something in me tightens up when I see her with Scag, looking at him, half-scared, half-admiring. And, if you must know, I don't like the sounds that come from their room during the afternoon and the evening. When I first heard it, I thought they were having a fight but now I know better. I can see Julie with that know-all smile, saying, "He's in bed with Carla. Where else?"

Does Carla really like him or is she just putting up with him? It takes two to tango, as Beth might say.

If it were just a feeling between Carla and me, a sort of friendship that's tipping into something else, I wouldn't worry—she's not going to leave Scag, and I've got one or two other problems—but, to judge from Julie's warning and Scag's coldness toward me, it's an open secret.

Even before that Saturday, I can hear the alarm bells ringing.

When we get back, Scag, Julie, Pete, John, and his new girlfriend, Danielle, are in the sitting room.

"Where's the dog?" goes Julie.

"The place was stinking with police," says Carla. "We pegged it."

"Ah." Julie drinks from the mug in her hand. "I thought we were going to have a pet."

At that moment, I'm glad that I haven't brought Jessie to the squat.

"Did they see you?" This is Scag. He's unshaven and

in a torn T-shirt. I find that I'm unable to look him in the eyes.

"Course not," says Carla. "I told you, we didn't hang around."

"There's going to be a party tonight," says Julie, looking at me. "Are you up for it, Nick?"

"Yes," I go. "Great. When does it start?"

Julie smiles. "Whenever," she says. "Late."

"We need more booze," says Pete. "I'll get some with John. You coming, Nick?"

I'm a bit startled by this. I've never been out with Pete or John, and I'm not sure I want to start now.

"If you want," I say, as unenthusiastically as I dare.

"It's a party," says Pete. "We've all got to help out either with money or doing a job. Got any money, have you?"

I glance toward Scag. He knows that the amount of work I've done this week has earned enough to buy a few bottles, if only he'd pay me.

He shrugs. Gee, thanks, Scag.

It must be eight o'clock when John knocks on my door. He's wearing a black T-shirt and jeans and, for the first time since I've met him, he seems to have washed his dark hair.

"Where do we buy the booze?" I ask.

"You'll see," goes John, swigging at a can of lager in the kitchen.

Pete's waiting in the corridor. "Ready to roll." He

smiles. There's something about the atmosphere that I don't like.

No one's looking me in the eye. It's like, Great party mood, right?

As I follow John and Pete down the stairs, Carla looks out of her room and beckons to me. She seems edgy.

"Good luck, Nick," she says loudly, adding under her breath, "watch your back, it's a setup."

I want to ask her more, but she's ducked back inside the bedroom.

Downstairs outside the front door, Pete's already in the driving seat of his old Cortina with the engine running. John jumps in the passenger seat. I'm going like, I'll get in the back then, shall I? but, since neither of them seems to feel like talking, I decide to hold the sarcasm and get in without a word.

We drive for, say, ten or fifteen minutes before we come to a street, where several of the shops are still open, their neon lights brightening up the darkness.

"I think I'm lost," goes Pete to John.

Pete, lost? This surprises me.

"Oh dear," says John, like a bad actor.

The car pulls up outside this big shop, selling all kinds of drink. Casually, John turns around to me and says, "We're looking for a place on Half Moon Lane. Ask the geezer in there for directions, will you, Nick?" He nods to the drinks shop, where a middle-aged Asian man is standing behind the till.

"And if he doesn't know," adds Pete, "ask him which

road we should take for Piccadilly. Just keep him talking, right?"

"We'll be doing a bit of shopping," John says. "If we come in, don't talk to us."

So I get out and go into the store. The Asian has that tired look of someone who spends his whole life working.

"You have to be eighteen to buy alcohol," he says as I approach the till.

I say, "I'm looking for Half Moon Lane. You couldn't point me in the right direction, could you?"

There's something entirely innocent about my voice and manner. Even after over ten days on the run, I seem to be a person to be trusted.

"Half Moon Lane," he says. "Now that's Streatham way, I think." From under the till, he takes out his street directory and starts thumbing through the pages.

"Ah yes," he mutters. "It's not close. It's a bit complicated. Are your parents taking you?"

"Yes," I go. "My dad."

We're both looking at the map when John and Pete wander in. I glance up, but, remembering my instructions, I return to the directory. "Left at the main road?" I ask.

There's a clinking of bottles behind us and, out of the corner of my eye, I see that John and Pete are filling two shopping baskets with spirits and wine. Suddenly I know what's going to happen but I'm powerless to act.

As if sensing my change of mood, the shopkeeper glances up—just as the boys pull open the door and, holding the baskets to their chests, run for it.

"Hey!" With surprising speed, the Asian leaps from behind the till and out of the door but Pete must have left the car engine running because, with a squeal of tires, they're off and away.

Thanks, guys.

I'm still in shock when the shopkeeper returns. He closes the door behind him and locks it.

"Nice friends you've got," he says, breathing heavily.

"Me?" My mouth is so dry I can hardly speak. "I never—I never met them."

"You can tell that to the police," goes the man, walking quickly to the phone while keeping a wary eye on me. "Don't try anything, all right." He glances to his left where, for the first time, I see a security camera. "You're on film anyway."

Like I was someone out of a dream, I take a deep breath and grab a bottle behind me, bringing it down with full force on the side of the till. Trying to keep the panic out of my voice, I scream, "Open the door or I"—desperately, I try to think what Scag would say—"or I bloody rearrange your face."

The man's eyes widen but he says, "Don't make it worse than it is or—"

"Do it!" I scream, jabbing in his direction with the broken bottle top.

"You're a bloody little fool," he says but, seeing the look in my eyes, he backs toward the door and unlocks it.

"Open it for me."

With a shrug, the Asian holds the door open. "Leave the broken bottle and we'll forget all—"

But, throwing the bottle to the ground, I hurl myself through the door and sprint down the street, my eyes stinging with tears. I dart down one side road, then another, before I reach a back road where there's a rubbish tip. Through the gloom, I look back down the street. All's quiet now, not even the distant siren of a police car.

I bury my face in my hands and sob in the darkness.

The party's in full swing by the time I get back to the squat. It's been a long walk and several times I catch myself thinking that I should forget it, disappear into the night, maybe go home.

I don't want to give them the satisfaction. I want to show them that I can look after myself, too.

Yes, the party's started all right. I can hear it from the end of the street. When I get to the front door, it's like the old house has taken on a life of its own. Music throbs through the air like a heartbeat.

I let myself in and the people in the hall—drinking, laughing, smoking—don't even give me a second look.

Then it's like, Excuse me but I happen to live here, as I push past them upstairs.

There's no sign of anyone I know so I make for my room. I need to lie down and think things over. The door's open and a couple of girls I don't recognize are lounging on my mattress, bottles of beer in their hands. They hardly look at me as I walk in.

"This is my room," I tell them.

One of the girls looks at me. "My room?" she says in a half-drunk way. "I thought everything was communal in this squat."

I'm not in the mood for a discussion about the concept of property. "I said it's my room."

"Charming," says the girl who spoke before, but she stands up, swigging from the bottle in her hand. Her friend gets to her feet, too. "Middle-class prat," she says as they both make for the door.

I wander over to the broken mirror and stare at myself for a while. My eyes are still red and there's a sheen of dirt on my face where the dust has stuck to the sweat.

Nick Morrison. Car thief. Straight man for a robbery. On the run. Dangerous. Do not approach this boy. I find myself laughing crazily at the idea.

Downstairs, the sound of voices and music seems to be getting louder. In my mind's eye, I see Pete, John, Julie, then Scag, maybe even Carla. We fitted old Nick up good and proper, eh? Won't be seeing him again. Great joke.

Without knowing quite what I'm going to do, I go downstairs.

John's in the kitchen talking to Pete, Danielle, and another girl. He does a double take like you see in sitcoms on the telly.

"Hey, you made it," he says eventually, moving away from the group so that they won't hear what we're saying.

"No bloody thanks to you," I hiss.

"Hey easy, right," he goes. "We thought you knew what was coming down. You were meant to do a runner when we did."

"You must think I'm stupid. You set me up."

"What?" This is Pete, who's wandered over to join us. "Why should we want to do that?"

"Anyway you got away," John says, changing the subject. "What happened?"

"I bottled him," I say casually. "In the face."

This lie seems to impress them both deeply.

"So now it's robbery with violence," I say. "You knew there were security cameras there, I suppose."

Pete shrugs like this was nothing new. "You don't say," he says, wide-eyed and sarcastic.

"Yeah," I go. "We're stars in our own video nasty." I'm just about to move off, when I ask casually, "Was this Scag's idea, setting me up?"

"I told you," John says. "We had no idea about—"

"Sure," I say, turning my back on them. There's an open bottle of beer on the kitchen table. I pick it up and take a swig, feeling ready to face Scag.

Who, as it happens, is nowhere to be found. I look in every room, in every corner where people are lying around, but there's no sign of Scag or Carla.

Eventually I try their bedroom. The door's locked. I knock.

Scag's voice tells me to get lost, or words to that effect.

So much for communal living. I go back to my room to plan for the future.

9

BOTTLE BOY

FEELINGS ARE STRANGE. YOU'D THINK THAT, WHEN I COME
around the next day, wake up in my bed a full-fledged
member of the criminal fraternity, surrounded by people
who are obviously happy to betray me to the police, my
first thoughts will be like, Lemme outta here, I'm back to
the bosom of the family.

But no. Partly because I can't stop thinking of the events
of the night, and partly because the music downstairs is
going at like a million decibels, I don't get to sleep until
about six in the morning. When I awake, late on Sunday
afternoon, my stomach is tight with anger. And here's the
sum total of my thoughts:

I HATE MY FAMILY.

It was the family that sent me away from home, the

98

family that started to crumble as soon as my back was turned, the family that called in the police when I asked them not to.

They don't understand. They haven't the faintest idea of what it's like to be me. They never did.

Everything seems insoluble. Stay here and I'll get betrayed again. Go home and I walk straight into the arms of the law, appear in court for armed robbery, and get sent to some prison-type school that makes Holton seem like heaven on earth.

It's their fault. I wanted none of this. I hope they realize that.

I've been awake a few minutes when there's a quiet knock on the door. Without waiting, Carla comes in wearing her best I'm-a-caring-human-being expression.

"Hey, Homebird," she says, standing by the mattress. "I heard what happened."

I shrug.

"I tried to warn you," she goes. "I had this feeling that they were trying to lose you."

"Feeling?" I go quietly. "You knew."

Carla shakes her head. "Scag was acting more strangely than usual. He took John aside last night and they must have discussed the setup. It's an old trick."

"I could have led the police back here."

Carla laughs. "John and Pete are more frightened of Scag than the police. You didn't really stab the shopkeeper, did you?"

"What do you think?" I say nastily, before adding, "I— just waved a bottle around a bit. Scared him."

"Tough guy."

I don't laugh.

"You missed the party," she says.

"I saw who I wanted to see."

"You didn't see me," Carla says quietly.

"You were busy." I avoid her eyes. "Busy in bed with the bastard who tried to shop me to the police."

"Nick," she says.

I ask her to leave, using John's favorite phrase, but, as soon as she's closed the door behind her, I feel bad.

"Carla," I say, but it's too late.

Something's changed in the squat. Apart from the fact that when, on Sunday evening, I go downstairs to get myself a bit of toast, the place is in like the most totally gross state that you can imagine—beer cans, bottles, dirty plates full of cigarette ends everywhere. There are even a few strange bodies littered about, on armchairs and on cushions in corners, partygoers who are still just about alive but won't be in any fit state to get out of the front door for some time.

I'm sitting at the kitchen table when Julie walks in, looking wrecked. I nod a greeting—and she looks away as if I'm not there.

Great, I think to myself. Now I'm the squat outcast.

"Hi, Julie," I say.

She puts the kettle on and stares out of the window, waiting for it to boil.

"How you doin'?" I try.

"Get lost," she goes, without turning around.

"Excuse me for breathing," I say, and shake my head at the shock of what I've just heard. It's as if Beth, the queen of cliché, has just hijacked my brain. Before I know it, I'll be saying, "You must be joking," or "Takes one to know one."

"You're bad news, you know that," Julie says suddenly. "I knew it as soon as I saw you. Totally bad news."

"Yeah, sorry about that. I suppose I should have let myself get arrested last night. That was really thoughtless of me."

"You don't fit in."

"Oh?" To tell the truth I can't think of an answer to this because, in my heart, I feel it's true. I'm just one of those people who never quite fit in. "Yeah, so who cares?" I finish lamely.

"You will," says Julie.

And I do, but not in the way that either of us expects.

It may be Sunday night and she may be coming down from a twelve-hour party, but Julie still goes out to work. It seems there's always a demand for what she has to sell.

I'm in bed asleep when she comes back at three or four in the morning. The first thing I know about it is when John wakes me, shaking my shoulder in a none-too-friendly way.

"You're wanted downstairs," he says.

"Wanted?" I mumble.

"Yeah," says John, straightening up and, as I begin to come around, I notice there's a strange, almost scared look in his eyes. "Something's happened."

As soon as I walk into the kitchen a few minutes later, barefoot and in my T-shirt and jeans, I know I have a problem. They're all there—Pete, John, Julie, and Carla are sitting at the table as if they're at one of my father's business meetings or something. Scag's standing by the stove, smoking a cigarette and smiling.

A smile on Scag's face is never good news.

In the middle of the kitchen table, there's a newspaper. Nothing unusual in that—often, on her way back from work, Julie calls in at the all-night store to buy a bar of chocolate and an early-morning edition of some trash paper.

But this one's unusual. Across the front page is the headline BOTTLE BOY. Underneath is the blurred picture of a wild-eyed kid in a shop, a broken bottle in his right hand—crazy, violent, the stuff of parents' nightmares.

You guessed it. The Bottle Boy is me.

My mouth dry, I pick up the paper, look at it for a moment or two, then throw it back onto the table.

"Fame at last," I say, but I can hear the tremor in my voice.

John reaches for the newspaper and starts to read from the bold type under my photograph.

"Saturday night. Battersea. A teenage thug threatens an elderly shopkeeper with a broken bottle while his two friends rampage through the shop, stealing bottles of alcohol before making their getaway.

"Except this teenage thug is different—he's Nicholas Morrison, the thirteen-year-old son of a respectable middle-class home. Thirteen days ago, Nicholas ran away from posh Holton School to live a life of crime.

"Nicky's merchant banker father, Gordon Morrison, a well-known figure in the city, last night made an impassioned plea for his son's return, and offered a 'substantial reward' for information on his whereabouts.

" 'There's no doubt that the boy in the security video is our son, Nicky,' said Mr. Morrison. 'I can only imagine he's fallen in with bad company and is being used by them. I am prepared to offer a substantial reward for information that will lead to Nicky's return. We want our son back.' "

John looks up from the paper. " 'Bad company,' eh, Nicholas? Do they mean us?" He glances back down at the page. "See Page Five for our Find Nicholas Morrison Action Line Number. Page Seven Comment—'What is happening to our children?' "

There's silence in the kitchen for like thirty seconds.

"The police will be around here within the day," says Julie. "Someone on the street will recognize the photograph, no problem."

"I'll go," I say quietly. "I'll leave now."

"And when they come here," Pete says, as if I hadn't

103

spoken, "they'll find John and me. We must be on that video, too."

"He always was trouble," mutters Julie.

I look at Carla but she just stares miserably down at her hands. Turning for the door, I say, "I'll get my stuff. I'm gone, right?"

"No." This is Scag in his quietest voice. "Stay. We'll work something out."

"I'd prefer to leave," I say, adding for Carla's benefit, "there's nothing for me here."

"I wasn't thinking of you," says Scag. "It's the rest of us I'm worried about. We have to survive out here when you're back with your Mummy and Daddy."

I look at him coldly. Scag, I sense suddenly, won't be a squatter for long. He's too bright, too ambitious to hang around the likes of John or Julie. Back in the real world, he'll find some way of using that power over people that he has to make money. Even now, I feel sorry for Carla.

"I need to think," he's saying. "Stay in your room for the moment. Don't go outside."

"If you're thinking I'm going to go to the police and tell them about you, I promise—"

Scag smiles again. "Go to your room, Nick. Be a good boy."

Call me an innocent fool, but I have no idea what's cooking even when, later that night, Scag opens the door to my room without knocking and says, "We've got a job, Nick."

"Me?"

"Who else?"

He watches wordlessly as I put on my jeans and T-shirt. "Car job?" I ask, trying to make conversation.

Dressed, I follow him downstairs. Apart from Carla, who's in the kitchen, no one seems to be around. It's when I catch a fleeting look on her face as our eyes meet that I realize that there's something odd about this job.

Regretful. Guilty perhaps. Yes, Carla's in on this.

She gives a little backward nod of the head as if she needs to tell me something, but Scag's walking purposefully down the stairs.

We're at the front door when I say casually, "Hey, I left my penknife behind. I'll be right with you, Scag."

Before he can say anything, I'm back up the stairs. In the kitchen, Carla gives a little smile of relief. Then holding a finger to her lips, she slips me a small book of matches.

"Nick, we've got to go." There's impatience in Scag's voice as he calls up the stairs.

"Matches?" I look at them in my hand. Then I see writing inside.

Once again, Carla puts a finger to her lips. Then she puts it to mine, like a finger kiss. It's about the sexiest thing that ever happened to me.

I'm off, down the stairs.

"Got the knife?" Scag asks.

"Mmm. Yeah, sure," I say.

I don't need to see what's written on the book of matches to know that this is no ordinary night's work. For a start, we're not walking as we usually do, but taking John's Cortina.

"How are we going to nick a car like this?" I ask.

Scag's driving carefully, glancing in the rearview mirror now and then. "You'll see," he says.

He's so preoccupied that, for a full five minutes, he doesn't even light up a cigarette. For Scag, who always has one on the go, this is truly weird. One mile, two miles—I can feel the matches in my pocket but, until he needs a light, I can't take them out.

We seem to be heading south.

In a moment of death-defying courage, I ask, "How did you get the name Scag?"

"That's what they called me at school."

He's driving easily now, one-handed, his right arm on the window.

"Scag," I go. "Strange name."

He says nothing.

"What's your real name then?"

He turns to me, raising his eyebrows, surprised at my daring.

"I won't tell anyone," I say.

He glances down at me and suddenly I know what's strange about Scag tonight. Before a job, he's tense like a tightrope, every part of him concentrating on his work. Then, when the car's nicked and we're heading toward his contact men, he becomes almost mellow, as if the prospect of money has eased his mind, relaxed him.

That's how he is now. Easy, relaxed. And yet he hasn't done the job.

Then I see it, even before I read Carla's note. Tonight it's not cars that's bringing Scag money, but me. The reward. I am the job.

Scag fumbles in his top pocket for a pack of cigarettes and, with a surge of relief, I pull out the book of matches Carla gave me.

"Arlo," he says. "That's what they called me." He darts me a laugh-and-you-die look. "Arlo."

"Nice name," I go, fumbling with the matches.

"Happy name," Scag says, leaning toward me so that I can light his cigarette. "My parents were hippies when I was born."

"My mum's like that," I go, suddenly ambushed by memories of home. "She sings old sixties songs in the kitchen."

Scag nods, not listening. I can tell that his own mind is back home with Mr. and Mrs. Scag, the hippies. I'm wondering if he misses them like I miss my parents.

The matches. Pretending to clean a thumbnail with a corner of the matchbook, I read Carla's note.

"They're turning you in for money. I'll leave your gear by the bins."

Of course. Just as I thought.

Pocketing the matches, I glance across and think, Gee, thanks a million, Arlo.

But how will he hand me over to the police? Scag is

wanted in connection with about a million crimes. As they say on the television, he is "known to the police."

He can't just leave me somewhere because he needs to collect the reward. Who else could do it? John and Pete would be recognized from the security video. Julie will have nothing to do with the police. I'm convinced that Carla wouldn't collect money in return for my captivity. Then I clock it. Scag's contact, his fence, the Mr. Respectable in the suburbs to whom he takes stolen cars. A perfect go-between. And that's why we're heading south.

Sometimes, just sometimes, things go your way. We're stopping for a traffic light when I see that, waiting at the lights and facing us, is a nightbus.

The lights change. I count to five as Scag moves forward, then, with the car still going at twenty or thirty, I open the passenger door and jump.

It hurts, as I hit the side of the road, turning an ankle on the pavement, but then I'm up and running back the way we came, after the nightbus. Trying to ignore the burning pain in my ankle I gain on the bus and swing onto it as it moves away from the lights.

At the back of my mind, I can hear the sound of squealing rubber as Scag tries to make the turn, but it's a narrow road and, by the time he's after us, there's a car between him and the bus.

As we take a corner and Scag briefly loses sight of us, I drop off the platform of the bus into the road and crouch between two parked cars.

The Cortina races by. At the next bus stop, Scag will be out of that car and into the bus, the only thing on his mind being the substantial reward that's slipping out of his hands. And I won't be there.

I like it. I like it a lot.

As soon as the bus and the Cortina have gone, I stand up. A stab of pain darts through my body from my ankle.

Easy, Tiger. Easy.

He'll be back soon, looking in dustbins, under cars.

Down the road, I notice that it gets darker, as if there aren't streetlamps there. I hobble down the quiet street, listening all the while for the sound of that Cortina.

Yes. My luck's turning. A park. A playground. Bushes. Trees. And no light. A runaway's paradise.

Up? Or down?

Nearby, there's a big old tree, whose lowest branches I can just about reach. I pull myself up and, trying to blank the pain in my ankle out of my mind, I climb up the tree so that I'm twenty, thirty feet above the ground and surrounded by leaves. Scag-proof.

The Cortina rolls by about ten minutes later, patrolling the road, but Scag must know he's lost me because he doesn't even stop in the park.

All the same, I spend the longest, most uncomfortable night in the tree. Apart from my throbbing ankle, a branch is cutting into the back of my leg. When about a million birds start celebrating the birth of a new day, I've had enough and slowly climb down. The earth feels good beneath my feet.

I'll leave your gear by the bins. Trying out my ankle as I make my way through the park in the half-light, I think back to the second part of Carla's message. What gear did she have that I needed?

Then I see it. She knew that I'd need my bag if I got away. She'd leave it outside the squat by the dustbins.

It's seven o'clock by the time I find a bus heading for Brixton, and the fare costs me the last bit of change I have in my pocket. One or two of the early-morning commuters give me curious looks and I'm praying they don't recognize me from the papers. Looking down at myself, I realize that I'm covered in leaves, my hands and clothes are dirty, and the laces on my bad foot are undone. You don't have to be Sherlock Holmes to deduce that I'm not exactly going to school for an early math lesson.

It's past eight by the time I reach Brixton and St. Mark's Road seems quiet. I watch the house where I've lived, where Carla's sleeping beside her lover, before I approach it.

There's no sign of life.

Behind the bins, my bag lies under a plastic bin-liner. I grab the bag and peg it, hopping painfully, down the road.

There's a warm autumn sun showing through the clouds by the time I reach a bench where I can check out my belongings.

Inside the bag, there are two spare shirts that I recognize as Carla's, an old blanket, a toothbrush, and—right at the bottom—a ten-pound note, wrapped inside a piece of paper. Carla's farewell message to me:

Homebird—
This is all I've got. Hope it helps. If the police catch
you, please don't lead them to the squat. I know
that you've got nothing to thank Scag for but he's
mixed-up. He's jealous of you and me!
Don't forget me. I won't forget you.
Love and XXXXXX,
Carla

I put the note and the money in my back pocket and wander down the street, not knowing where to go next, not caring really.

Home's not the greatest idea, that's for sure. Not now that the police are after me.

Something in me wants to cry but I'm so sad that I feel I'm never going to cry again. Maybe that's difficult to understand, but it's true.

I should be thinking of the future. Or of my family. But I'm not, I'm thinking of Carla and her XXXXXX.

Maybe I'll see her again. Maybe, back in the real world.

10

RIVER SCUM

HERE'S AN ODD THING.
Many of the people hurrying past me on their way to work are carrying the newspaper with my face on the front but, the fact is, if one of them grabs me and says, "You are the Bottle Boy and I claim my substantial reward," I wouldn't care. I'm too tired to bother about ducking and diving anymore. I'm hungry, and my foot aches.

But they don't. These people going to work are like something out of *Invasion of the Zombie Commuters*. Their eyes are totally glazed and dead. I'm thinking like, No way am I ever going to work in a so-called normal job when I leave school. Then I laugh quietly to myself. At this rate, the only job I'll be doing is sewing mailbags in the local jail somewhere.

I must have been walking for an hour or so, just thinking and getting more and more depressed about the mess I've made of my life, because after a while I notice I've reached the river by Waterloo.

For a while I watch the zombies as they cross the river, with their quick what's-the-boss-going-to-say steps, but my ankle's throbbing now, so I go down some steps and sit under the bridge to think.

About twenty yards away, silhouetted against the light, there's an old woman, singing a song over and over again, shaking coins in a plastic cup in her hand. People walk by, now and then glancing at her or muttering something to one another. She just keeps on with this song about you are my sunshine.

I begin to feel seriously sorry for myself as I sit there, listening to the old girl singing, while the rest of the world goes about its business. There's nothing more depressing, I think, than seeing the older generation giving it the old stiff-upper-lip when there's absolutely nothing to be cheerful about.

I'm so deep in thought that, when I hear the tinkle of a coin hitting the stone ground, it takes a few seconds for me to realize what's happening. There's a pound coin between my feet. I look up and see this smartly dressed woman clip-clopping away on her high heels, closing her bag as she walks.

She thinks I was begging!

I'm still wondering what to do with the coin when a

middle-aged businessman fishes deep into his trouser pocket and, avoiding my eyes as if I'm not there, leans down to put some change in front of me.

"Excuse me," I'm going, but before I can explain that I don't want his money, he's off like he's really embarrassed by what he's done.

The old lady stops singing at this point and starts walking toward me, still shaking the few coins in her plastic cup as if the beat's continuing in her head. She stands in front of me and I see she's not that old, but the street grime on her face, hands, and clothes makes it difficult to judge her age. She has these glasses on, an old cardigan over her thin shirt, and what looks like soccer socks down around her ankles under a pair of sandals.

"This is my patch," she says.

"Sorry."

"Don't sorry me." I notice her looking at my pile of coins and I feel really guilty. "Just sod off out of it."

"I was enjoying your song," I say, which is a bit of a lie, as it happens.

"Yeah, well," goes the woman. "You can still sod off."

As she speaks, I'm picking up the coins. I stand up, my body aching from lack of sleep, and drop them into her plastic cup. The woman seems a bit less hostile now. "How old are you?" she asks.

"Thirteen."

She shrugs, like it's not her problem if I'm thirteen or thirty. Then, seeing a group of people walking toward us,

114

she starts singing again, louder than ever, "The other night, dear, while I lay sleeping—"

On an impulse, I take the plastic cup from her and shake it in time to the song. A couple of girls, one of whom looks a bit like my father's lover, Jo, slow down and look at us. For a moment I think they recognize me from the newspaper but then they slow down and, as if at a given signal, open their bags, and each puts some coins in the cup.

I'm thinking like, A great team is born. Me and the sunshine lady—since she won't tell me her name, I think of her as Sunny.

"You are my sunshine," she goes.

Shake, shake, I go.

Maybe we'll release a single one day.

By the time the rush hour dies down, we've made a few pounds. I'm just thinking that if I hear that damned song one more time I'll scream, when Sunny stops, peers into the plastic cup, and says, "Tea break."

She opens an old green canvas bag that's on the ground behind her and carelessly chucks the money into it. Picking the bag up, she moves off like someone who just remembered she's got an appointment elsewhere.

I stand there for a moment, uncertain as to whether I'm invited.

"Tea break!" This time she shouts it over her shoulder. It's not like the warmest invitation I've ever received but

I'm hungry now and there's nowhere else to go, so I follow.

The café where Sunny takes me has condensation on the windows so thick that you can't see the street outside. It's full of people and cigarette smoke and there's a smell of bacon that reminds me of the fry-ups that Carla used to make for Scag and me after we had done a job.

I wonder how Carla is now.

"Move yer arse, darling." A woman of about 150 and carrying two bulging plastic bags is standing behind me as I wait for Sunny to find us a place.

"Sorry," I go, snapping out of my thoughts of Carla.

"Who's your new boyfriend, darling?" someone asks as we sit down. I smile politely like, Big joke.

At first, while Sunny tells me about herself as we eat a breakfast of fat with a bit of bacon and egg in there somewhere, it's interesting. Her husband was a fighter pilot killed in the Battle of Britain, she says. They must have been very rich because she lived in this big house with a gardener and butler. She drove an ambulance during the war and used to save about five lives every day. Unfortunately she had to move out of the house when she discovered the gardener was a German spy in league with the Devil.

I'm like, "Oh, really?"

It takes a while, because I tend to believe what people say but, by the time Sunny tells me the reason she's living on the streets is because the government, which is also in league with the Devil, is looking for her and that she knows something about what they're doing to water, something

116

that is so secret she can't even tell me, I'm thinking, This is a serious crazy we've got here.

Suddenly she stops talking and, her fork laden with a dripping egg poised in front of her mouth, she suddenly asks, "What do they call you then?"

That's nice, I'm thinking. She won't tell me her name, but she needs to know mine. "Nick," I say.

"*What?*" Her hand is shaking. "What did you just say?"

"Er." And suddenly I remember something I was once taught in history or religion. "Nick" used to be the name given to the Devil. "Old Nick," they used to call him if he ever existed, which he didn't.

Sunny's looking at me through narrowed eyes.

"Dick," I go quickly. "You can call me Richard if you like."

"Hmm." She goes back to eating her breakfast, occasionally giving me this really suspicious look.

"Why can't you tell me your name?" I ask, hoping to lighten up the atmosphere.

Sunny gives an odd, that-old-trick chuckle. She taps the side of her nose confidentially. "Wouldn't you like to know," she says. "Have you got fillings?"

I'm thinking like, Now what? "No," I say, "I'm a real dentist's pet."

"Good," goes Sunny. "They use fillings to tune into your brain, you know."

Jeez. Lemme outta here.

Except that there's nowhere for me to go. When Sunny

gets up from the table, reaching into her canvas bag for some coins to pay for our breakfast, I find myself following her.

"I'll show you where we sleep," she goes, once we're outside the café. "You got a blanket?"

"A thin one in my bag." It's the first time that it has occurred to me that Sunny sleeps rough and on the streets.

She leads me about half a mile down the river to a sort of settlement in a yard behind a car park. Littered in every corner are cardboard boxes, sometimes in the form of little shelters, sometimes laid flat on the ground. Ignoring Sunny, I walk slowly past a man lying on his back under a blanket. He has a gray beard and a dark, grimy skin but his face seems peaceful as he sleeps. In his arms, he's cradling a bottle as if it were a baby.

I look across the yard. A tall, unshaven man, as thin as anyone I've ever seen, has wandered over to where Sunny has put down her bag beside a little hutch of cardboard. In the autumn sun, he talks to her but Sunny seems to be ignoring him.

After the thin man has gone, I walk over to her.

"Home," she says, arranging a blanket before sitting down at the entrance to her hutch. "What's the matter? Seen a ghost?"

"No," I say faintly.

"There's a supermarket down the road. We'll get you some cardboard."

"What about blankets?"

Without a word, Sunny stands up and walks away. Awkwardly, I follow her. By the road, there's a van in which I can see a woman with short hair and glasses reading a newspaper.

"Don't go to the hostel, right?" says Sunny as we walk toward the van. "They try to get you to go but it's a trick."

The woman in the van smiles as we approach.

"We need a blanket," goes Sunny. "Boy here needs a blanket."

"Just arrived?" the woman asks.

I nod.

"There's a hostel for youngsters, you know. I can take you there."

"No, thank you," I go. The fact is the idea of going into a tramp hostel doesn't exactly appeal to me.

"I call by every day." The woman gets out of the van, opens the back, and hands me a blanket. "If you want any help I'm here, right?"

"Thanks." I take the blanket.

"I'm Jill. What's your name?"

"Dick," I say, backing away. "I'll let you have the blanket back when I've finished with it."

"By the way," I ask Sunny as we make our way to the supermarket to find me a house, "what's wrong with the hostel?"

She smiles confidently, then looks around to check that no one can hear her as we walk along. "It's run by the Devil."

"Ah." Of course. Silly me.

That night I see Dad.

We've been working around Sunny's daily routine, which involves singing "You Are My Sunshine" from eight until ten under the bridge and from four until six down in the Waterloo underground, and lounging around the settlement for the rest of the day.

We've just done the evening stint and I swear I never want to hear that song again. But the Old Girl and the Ragamuffin act that we've been putting on for commuters seems to do the trick. I've had to empty the coins in the plastic cup three or four times and an embarrassed-looking older man even gave us a fiver.

I'm climbing the steps out of the underground into the main station when suddenly, without even knowing I've seen him, I sense Dad's presence. First I think he must be among the commuters but then I look behind the stream of people. There, walking slowly by a snack van, is my father. He's looking at a couple of boys who are sprawled on the ground against the wall with a small piece of cardboard in front of them. I've seen them at the station earlier in the day—HOMELES PLESE HELP, their sign reads.

Sunny is walking toward Dad but I like freeze. He looks up from the dossers toward where I'm standing, jostled by the commuters.

Easy, Tiger. I'm torn between going to him and running

back down the stairs. Dad looks terrible. There's no way that he's been to work with his suit in that state. His eyes have a vacant, sleepless look. He seems gray, old.

For seconds, I'm unable to move. I close my eyes and it's as if I'm drowning as people rush past me. When I open them, the station's all blurred from tears. I wipe my face and look toward where Dad was standing. He's gone, like a ghost or a dream.

"Hamburger, Dick?" Sunny asks me.

"Yes," I go.

"Here, are you all right?"

"Fine."

You discover things living on the street, things that you don't see in the comfort of your own home. There's a sort of wisdom—

Now, whoa there—check that major cliché attack. Like the wisdom of the streets, right? The pitiful little urchins with the strangely old eyes, the wonderful leather-skinned old girl who understands life's deepest mysteries? There, among the cardboard boxes and winos and runaways, the great, glowing secret of What It's All About?

Er, no.

I'm still in a daze from seeing my father when Sunny leads me back to the settlement. As night falls and there's the beginning of an autumn chill, a group of kids—four boys and one girl, all about my age or a bit younger—appear out of the shadows. They're carrying boxes and bits of driftwood from the banks of the river. Soundlessly they build a fire in the middle of the yard and set light to it.

Attracted by the warmth, figures appear from out of the shadows and gather around the crackling fire, not saying much, just staring into the flames.

"All right, put that out."

The first great truth I learn from the streets is that, when you're without a home, you get less respect from the rest of the world than a stray dog would.

The fire's been going about fifteen minutes or so when two policemen appear. They stand about ten yards back from the fire. "Put the———fire out." The older policeman swears a lot as he tells us we're creating a fire hazard. Among the more polite names he calls us is "river scum."

There's a bit of muttering among the older dossers, but when the policemen move closer and threaten to "take us in," we start pulling wood from the fire and letting it die down.

At one point, the long overcoat of the tall, thin man I saw earlier catches light, and he dances around shaking it off, then stamping on it. This makes the policemen laugh as they move off, their work done.

"Should have let it burn," one of them says to the other. "Would have been one less bit of scum to worry about."

A couple of the kids are looking at me after the police

have gone, their hard, flick-knife eyes shining out of their grim faces.

"We're going working," one of them says to me. "Wanna come?"

I shake my head. "No, thanks."

"Be a laugh." The older boy has dark, straight hair that falls forward over his eyes. "Show you around."

But these kids frighten me. Trying to look casual, I shrug, turning away from them and walking back to where Sunny's settling down. She may be crazy but at least she's not dangerous. I hear them laughing contemptuously.

Around the yard, there's the sound of Cardboard City at night: drunken mumbling, snatches of songs, raised voices, swearing, as some kind of argument breaks out.

Another lesson of the streets: The farther away from home you are, the more you talk about it.

I sit by Sunny's hutch, my blanket wrapped around her shoulders as she talks on and on about the home in Surrey, the butler, the green, the big hall, the husband who's like Mr. Perfect, sunny afternoons trimming the roses to the sound of birdsong, croquet hoops on the lawn, cocktails on the veranda.

I'm not stupid—I know this is fantasyland but it seems to keep Sunny going through the cold night and, the fact is, it keeps my mind off my problems. It's eleven or twelve by the time Sunny stops talking. Then, as if I'm not there, she turns over and is asleep within seconds.

It's cold. That's my third lesson of street life. A blanket

isn't enough. The chill of the paving stones rises through the thin cardboard. It's a still night, but even the slightest breeze makes me shiver.

One. Two. Three. I hear a distant bell chime. Four.

My bones aching, my eyes hurting from lack of sleep, I get up to walk around the settlement. Although some of the sleepers snore drunkenly, now and then crying out in their sleep, it's as quiet as it's going to get in Cardboard City.

I'm sitting on the wall of the Thames when suddenly I'm aware of two figures approaching. I slip down behind a bench. It's the two policemen I saw earlier.

They enter the yard. Then, slowly making their way around the circle, they shine their flashlights into the face of each of the sleepers.

There are drowsy curses, even from Sunny when they reach her. Shining their flashlights on my blankets and cardboard they say something to each other that I can't catch.

Are they looking for me? Does this happen every night? Standing up from behind the bench after the policemen have gone, I know that the time has come to make my move.

11

BUSTED

THE NEXT MORNING, SUNNY AND I MAKE SOME SERIOUS cash during the morning rush hour with the disastrous result that it's "You Are My Sunshine" right through to ten-thirty. By the time she sings the final tuneless, croaky-voiced chorus, I'm about ready to throw myself in the Thames.

That song, please, I don't even want to think about it.

So we hit the café for breakfast late and with Sunny in a really up mood.

"In good voice today, I was," she says, slurping her second cup of tea.

"Yes," I say. From the way she's talking, anyone would think she had just had a million encores at the Festival Hall. "Why d'you always sing that song?" I ask in a rash moment.

She looks at me, surprised by the question. "They like it, don't they."

"Maybe they just feel—" I stop myself from hinting that anyone might feel sorry for her.

"Tried another song once," she says. " 'Pack Up Your Troubles in Your Old Kit Bag.' Disaster." A distant, crazed smile appears on her face, which gives me a bad feeling about what's going to happen next. "Pack . . . up . . . yer . . . teroubles . . . in an old . . ."

I look away as she starts singing, making like, She's nothing to do with me, right? I have something important to tell her but now, as everyone in the café stares in our direction, doesn't seem quite the right moment.

It's a warm autumn day and later, as we sit watching the river before going to Waterloo Station for the evening shift, I try to explain my idea.

"The thing is," I say, "I'm a runaway. In fact the police are looking for me. I was in the papers."

Sunny nods, blinking through the dusty lenses of her glasses.

"There's a reward for information leading to my being found," I go.

"Oh yeah." This is not said with great interest.

"And you're going to get it," I say.

"Eh?"

"It's the answer," I say more urgently. "You phone the police. I turn myself in. You get the reward."

"Reward?"

Somehow I sense that I'm not getting through. "A substantial reward, the paper said. It could be a thousand pounds—enough to get you away from here. Maybe you could go back down to Surrey."

The color of Sunny's face seems to have darkened. "Get thee behind me, Satan," she says quietly.

"No, you're getting it wrong," I say, desperate to get the conversation away from her favorite subject. "I don't want anything in return—"

"The evil one sends me children now," she says with rising hysteria in her voice. "Silver-tongued infants to buy my soul. Oh cunning, oh sly—"

I'm like, Hey, easy, Tiger, I was only trying to get you away from this place. "So you're not that interested in the reward?" I try.

With great dignity, she stands up, looking away from me as she picks up her canvas bag. "He held my plastic cup," she says in a distant, tragic voice. "Satan held my plastic cup."

"I'm sorry I mentioned it." I'm five paces behind her as she makes for the station like an old tug heading out of the harbor. Muttering to herself, she refuses to even acknowledge that I'm there.

It definitely doesn't help a working relationship if your partner happens to think that you're the Devil. Every time she stops at one of her pitches on the underground, she glances at me, then hurries on as if there's no way she's

127

going to break into song while Satan's around. In the end, I reach into my pocket and, while she's looking away from me in disgust, I slip the ten-pound note in her bag.

"See you," I go. "Thanks for all your help."

I walk away. I'm climbing the steps up to the station when I hear down the echoing corridor, "You are my sunshine, my only sunshine." From this distance, it sounds almost good.

There's just enough change in my pocket for a hamburger, so I wander along to a McDonald's on the street by the station and order a Big Mac.

Sitting in the brightly lit room, it occurs to me that eating has begun to play a less important part in my daily routine. Breakfast in the morning, maybe a ham sandwich at night, and that's my diet since I left the squat. In a mirror across the room, I catch a glimpse of a ratlike character, his hair matted, his clothes dark and grimy and, just as I'm thinking, They'll let anyone into this place, I see that it's me.

My sunken, wary eyes don't look great. My skin looks loose and unhealthy. I feel pretty foul, too—it's as if my teeth have grown fur and, as for my underpants, they haven't been washed for so long, they're as stiff as cardboard. If I smell as bad as I look, I'm in deep trouble.

I find myself thinking more and more of that reward. Whether it comes from Dad or the newspaper or the police makes no difference. If all it takes is for this scrawny body of mine to return home, then I want that money to find its way from the cozy, secure world of right and wrong

128

and fridges and table manners and TV every night into the cold outside where the only success is to survive another day.

It isn't going to be easy, as my attempt to make Sunny understand had shown—but I can try.

I must have drifted into some weird dream, or even fallen asleep, because by the time I make my move out of the McDonald's, it's dark outside and the remains of my hamburger are congealed and cold. One or two people look at me as I walk slowly out of the joint but I stare them out, confident that no one will recognize the Bottle Boy from the newspaper.

The rush hour's past now and, when I reach the underground, skipping through the barrier, Sunny has left her pitch and headed home. She'll be back by the riverside now. I take the train to Brixton.

A blue light's flashing at the end of the street, but then after nightfall there's almost always a blue light flashing somewhere in Brixton. Police, fire, ambulance—we're like the best customers the emergency services ever had.

My plan's simple—to wait until Scag and the rest of them have gone out to work, then to see Carla. She'll have to make the call, telling the police where they can find me, and her money problems will be over.

Homebird, she used to call me. Well, I'd be home soon.

I'm so deep in thought that I'm almost in St. Mark's Road when I notice there's a small crowd of people at the junction with the main street. Making my way through them, I find there's a white tape barring the way and that a police car is parked diagonally across the road.

"What's going on?" I ask a young guy who's standing, his arm around his girlfriend, as if they were waiting for the show to begin.

"Car chase," he says. "The police are just about to go into the house down there." He points to the squat, some hundred yards away. Outside, on the street, there's another police car with its blue light flashing.

"Joyriders," says his girlfriend. "They crashed their car on the corner and legged it back to the house."

Now I can see, beyond the house, John's Cortina skewed into the middle of the road, a great dent in its side.

"Nice parking," I go weakly.

I'm just trying to work out how to get closer to the house without being spotted by the law when there's the sound of more sirens approaching. A police constable standing by the tape walks briskly back to his car, takes out a megaphone, and, as three more police cars and a van draw up, it's like, "Please clear the road. This is a police operation. Do not obstruct the officers in the course of their duties."

The crowd backs onto the pavement. It's my chance. As everyone's watching the police move in, I hop over a wall and duck and dive my way through front gardens until I'm no more than thirty yards away from the front door of the squat.

Hidden behind some dustbins, I see it all, lit up by the

blue lights as if it were some kind of nightmare.

By now it seems like scores of police are moving toward the front door. For a moment, they stand on the steps, almost as if posing for a photograph. Then someone shouts something and the front two men put their shoulders to the door. It takes two, three shoves before, with a loud crack, the hinges break. Truncheons drawn, the men in blue swarm into the house.

It doesn't take long. There are sounds of shouting, a scream. Then John appears at the front door, held by two policemen, one of whom is pulling him by his hair while the other holds his arms behind his back. Screaming abuse at them, John is thrown into the back of the police van.

After that, it's a procession. Pete, then Danielle. Julie comes out, fighting like a crazed cat.

I'm breathing heavily by now. Is it possible, just possible that Scag and Carla are out for the evening? I try to see them on line for the cinema but it doesn't work.

Then something attracts my attention, a movement in the rooftop shadows high above the street. A small window—it must be in the attic—open slowly and a figure wriggles through it. For a moment, his silhouette shows up against the brickwork as he shimmies silently along a ledge, then onto the top of the roof.

Scag. There's no mistaking him. Praying to myself, I keep my eyes trained on that tiny window waiting, praying for Carla. As cool as a fox eluding the hounds, Scag glides along the ridge of the roof, jumps the gap leading to the neighboring house, and, as he lands, slides down the slates on the far side and out of sight.

Ahead of the game as usual, Scag's away and free.

The small attic window stares out onto the street like a dark eye. For one, two minutes I watch it, thinking of Carla. Then suddenly I see her.

She's not at the window but at the front door. There's a policeman behind her but, unlike the others she's not struggling or fighting. For a moment, she looks up and down the street, as cool as someone looking to see whether the milkman has called.

The policeman touches her on the shoulder and, with a quiet dignity that makes me want to stand up and cheer, Carla walks down the steps and climbs into the back of the van.

"Reverse charge call."

"Where to?"

I give the operator my parents' number.

A couple of rings and my mother picks up, sleepy but alert. It's three in the morning and, although I've been pacing the streets of South London since they took Carla away, I'm shivering with cold.

"Call from a Stockwell pay phone," I hear the operator saying. "Will you accept the call?"

There's this sort of gasp.

"Yes, yes," says Mum.

"It's me." Something odd seems to have happened to

my voice and this comes out as a sort of croak.

"Nicky, oh my God, where are you, darling?"

I hear my father's voice in the background.

"It doesn't matter where I am," I say. "I'll come home but I must know something first. A friend of mine called Carla Johnson has just been arrested at a squat in Brixton."

"Yes," my mother says. "We were told that the two boys you were filmed with in the wine shop had been seen. The last we heard the police had arrested them."

"I need to know that Carla's not being charged with anything."

"Nicky." There's a tremble in Mum's voice. "What's all this got to do with our little family?"

"She's innocent, Mum."

"Are you all right?"

"I'll ring back in ten minutes," I go. "Do this and I'll be home in time for breakfast."

To tell the truth, I find this total cliché touch-guy act a problem talking to my mum, but I know that the only way I can carry it off is to pretend it isn't me making the call, but a hero in someone else's movie.

After hanging up, I walk around the block a few times. Then, maybe twenty minutes later, I call again, reverse charge. My mother answers.

"Any news?" I ask.

"Dad spoke to the detective inspector in charge of your case," Mum says quietly. "It appears that this Carla person was picked up tonight. They've spoken to her and are keeping her overnight." Mum's voice sounds wobbly again, as if she's trying to keep the hysterics at bay. "As long as nothing incriminating is found at the house, she'll be released tomorrow."

"You promise?" I say. "It's not a trick."

"No."

I'm thinking that maybe I should hear it from the police themselves. If nothing else, life on the run has shown me that you can trust nobody. In the distance, I hear my mother's voice. I realize that I'm holding the telephone receiver to my stomach.

"What?" I say, pulling myself together.

"Where are you?" Mum sounds panicky.

"Oh." I look at the address in the telephone kiosk. I read it out.

"We're on our way," says Mum.

I must be more tired than I thought.

As I put the receiver down, my legs buckle. I lean against the plastic wall of the kiosk and like ease myself to the ground. I hug my knees to my chest. Footsteps passing and fading but no one stops. I'm so tired. My head sags forward. . . .

"Nicky."

I look up to see Mum standing before me. Behind her, Dad and Beth are getting out of the car.

"Easy," I'm saying. "Eas—"

Mum crouches in front of me and puts her arms around my shoulders, resting her lips on my lank hair. I can hear Beth crying.

"Come on, old boy," my father's saying. "In the car."

"Nicky." Mum's like totally wracked with sobs.

"Easy—" It's no good, there's something stuck in my throat. The words won't come out.

I feel these arms picking me up and, this is really odd but, as I slip into unconsciousness, I'm aware of the familiar smell of my father's body.

"Dad."

Then I'm out of it.

12

CLICHÉ EVER AFTER

THAT'S TWO MONTHS AGO; THIS IS NOW.

Several things have happened, not all of them good.

My father has moved out. Not with Jo, who ditched him, perhaps for a man who doesn't ruin a perfectly good dinner date by running out of the restaurant in pursuit of his son. I guess I should feel sorry for Dad, but I don't.

His secretary. I mean, *please*.

All the same, now he lives in a neat little flat not far from here. I see him two or three times a week and, weird as it may seem, I get on better with him these days now that I'm not caught in the cross fire between him and Mum. He's quieter now, and has been known to listen when someone else is speaking, as if living alone has proved to him that you don't have to be a total dictator to be taken seriously. He even gave that reward to some charity for the homeless which, believe me, is like the ultimate miracle.

My mother has changed, too. It wasn't the most terrible shock in the world, she explained to me, to discover that "your father," as she now calls Dad, was seeing someone else. In fact, she knew all along. Sometimes I wonder why they couldn't be honest with each other and with Beth and me, why I had to run away to bring it all out in the open.

This week she's gone to a concert with some old divorced guy with buckteeth and a totally patronizing manner. It's like, No Mum, please, not him, but since he dropped her back home at 10:15, maybe this isn't going to be the romance of the century after all.

Here's hoping.

Beth's in love with some toe-rag from college. You really don't want to know about it. Just imagine the biggest cliché in the history of humankind, then double it, and you'll have an idea of what my sister's like these days. We still have arguments, but when it gets really bad I remember that it was Beth I turned to first when I was on the run. She's not bad, for a sister.

I am not in prison. There were a few sticky moments after I came home, but when John surprised everyone, probably himself included, by telling the police that I wasn't involved in the wine store robbery, I was told that all charges would be dropped if I apologized to the Asian man I had threatened with a bottle. This, I swear, was the most embarrassing conversation of my entire life.

Talking of prison, it was decided not to send me back to Holton. These days, I'm back in my old school, but Paul and Quadir have promised to give me regular reports from hell. I have not received a welcome home card from Pringle, or even from Wattsy.

Yesterday, I'm walking Jessie in the park when Marlon comes on over to see me. As usual, I ask if he's seen Carla.

"Nope," says Marlon. "But we had a note from her yesterday."

"Where is she then?" I ask, trying to sound casual.

"Didn't say. Holed up with Scag somewhere."

"Hmmm." It's like total heartbreak time. I want to die. "Good old Scag," I say, looking away.

"Oh," goes Marlon, as if he's suddenly remembered something. "She sent us this to give you." He reaches into a back pocket and pulls out a crumpled envelope marked, "Nick—PRIVATE."

After Marlon's gone, I sit on a park bench and, savoring the moment, open the envelope slowly and read:

Hey, Nick—
I wanted to thank you for what you did for me after the bust. You're a true friend.
Things are hot right now but, believe me, I'll be keeping in touch with you.

Grow quick, Homebird. I'll be waiting for you.
All my love,
Carla

I stare across the park to where we once walked hand in hand to kid the police lookout man we were lovers. I'm remembering Carla's words. That was for him, this is for me.

Grow quick.

I'm like, Just try and stop me.

Calling Jessie, I push the note into my back pocket and make for home.